His husky voice was dreamy, and when their eyes met, her mind went blank. It felt good being with a suave, charming man who smelled divine and showered her with compliments, and Haley wanted to spend the rest of the night hanging out with him.

"Can I ask you something?"

Curious, Haley nodded her head. "Sure. Ashton, what is

rst."

"I haven't met the right person yet. You?"

"Yesterday I would have said the same thing, but I've recently had a change of heart. I'm interested in a beautiful charity CEO, but I don't want to scare her off by revealing my true feelings." Ashton winked. "I'm pacing myself. It's only our first date."

Their eyes met.

"I had fun tonight," he said, "and I'd love to see you again."

Haley moistened her lips with her tongue. "To discuss the Aunt Penny Foundation?"

"No," he said calmly. "To wine you and dine you."

Dear Reader,

I love writing miniseries, so when my fabulous editor asked if I would be interested in writing the third book in the Millionaire Mogul series, I said, "Heck yeah! Count me in!" Brainstorming sessions with Yahrah St. John (*Miami After Hours*) and Sherelle Green (*A Miami Affair*) really got my creative juices going, and I think we did an awesome job on the series. I hope you'll agree.

Ashton Rollins can't get Haley Adams out of his mind. So he shows up unannounced at her office early one morning, persuades her to have dinner with him at his Fisher Island estate and turns on the charm the moment she steps foot on his property. And that's not all. He wines and dines her, whisks her away to Venezuela for a romantic weekend and kisses her with such warmth and tenderness she melts in his arms. Haley only wishes Ashton would open up about his past, and when an explosive secret threatens their happily-ever-after, she must decide if their love is worth fighting for.

Look for *Seduced by the Tycoon at Christmas* this holiday season. It's the final book in the Morretti Millionaire series, and I'm confident you're going to love it. You can visit me at www.pamelayaye.com, and send me emails at pamelayaye@aol.com.

All the best in life and love,

Pamela Yaye

Secret Miami Nights

Pamela Yaye

Recycling programs for this product may not exist in your area.

ISBN-13: 978-0-373-86509-3

Secret Miami Nights

For questions and comments about the quality of this book please contact us at CustomerService@Harlequin.com.

HARLEQUIN®
www.Harlequin.com

Printed in U.S.A.

Pamela Yaye has a bachelor's degree in Christian education. Her love for African American fiction prompted her to pursue a career in writing romance. When she's not working on her latest novel, this busy wife, mother and teacher is watching basketball, cooking or planning her next vacation. Pamela lives in Alberta, Canada, with her gorgeous husband and adorable but mischievous son and daughter.

Books by Pamela Yaye

Harlequin Kimani Romance

Pleasure for Two
Promises We Make
Escape to Paradise
Evidence of Desire
Passion by the Book
Designed by Desire
Seduced by the Playboy
Seduced by the CEO
Seduced by the Heir
Seduced by Mr. Right
Heat of Passion
Seduced by the Hero
Seduced by the Mogul
Mocha Pleasures
Seduced by the Bachelor
Secret Miami Nights

Visit the Author Profile page
at Harlequin.com for more titles.

Leave your past in the past, or it will destroy you.
Live for what today has to offer,
not for what yesterday has taken away.
—Author Unknown

Chapter 1

"Welcome home, Mr. Rollins." Cap in hand, the suit-clad limousine driver bowed at the waist and nodded his bald, shiny head in greeting. "It's an honor to meet you."

Ashton Rollins was beat, exhausted after his ten-hour flight from Frankfurt, but he read the driver's name tag and shook his outstretched hand. "York, the pleasure is all mine."

A proud smile exploded onto York's wide, tanned face. Racing around to the passenger-side door, he yanked it open and gestured at the backseat with a dramatic flourish of his hands.

Embarrassed by the driver's effusive behavior, Ashton noticed the employees on the tarmac at Miami International Airport's General Aviation Center were staring at him. He was the Chief Operating Officer of his family's business, Rollins Aeronautics, not a head of state, and unlike his father, Alexander, he didn't like people fussing over him.

Lowering his head, he ducked inside the limousine and

rested his briefcase at his feet. Ashton unbuttoned his tailored suit jacket and made himself comfortable. A week ago, he'd traveled to Frankfurt to attend the Aerospace Expo, and had worked nonstop while in the bustling metropolis. He'd arrived at the airport twenty minutes earlier by corporate jet, and the landing had been so rough his head was still spinning. Ashton would have preferred piloting his private plane to travel, but these days he had no time for his favorite hobby.

Ashton unzipped his briefcase, took out his tablet and turned it on. But he didn't review his weekly schedule. His thoughts were on Haley Adams—the bubbly, effervescent CEO he'd been introduced to weeks earlier at the Millionaire Moguls meeting. For five years, Ashton had been president of the exclusive club. It was as discreet as it was powerful, and members couldn't buy their way in—they had to be invited. The name of the organization was officially Prescott George, but the media called them the Millionaire Moguls. Ashton hated the moniker. The Moguls were more than just wealthy businessmen: they did good work. They provided college scholarships to needy students, funded inner-city organizations and changed lives.

Pride filled him at the thought of how much they'd accomplished. Every year, the Moguls chose a charity to support, and this year they'd selected The Aunt Penny Foundation. The organization would reap the profits from the Moguls' seventy-fifth anniversary party and charity gala to be held at Ashton's Fisher Island estate at the end of August, but he wasn't going to wait six weeks to see Haley Adams. Screw that. He wanted to see her now. Today. Before one of the other moguls swooped in and stole her away. The twenty-eight-year old CEO was a magnet, the type of woman who attracted male attention wherever she went, and he couldn't risk someone else winning her heart.

Ashton remembered with astounding clarity the day they'd met. Her smile had stayed with him from the moment he'd laid eyes on her, and weeks later he was still thinking about her. Ashton didn't know why. They'd only talked for a couple minutes. Haley was supposed to give a presentation on behalf of The Aunt Penny Foundation, but she'd received an emergency phone call and promptly left. He'd made inquiries about her after the meeting wrapped up, and learned from her colleague Becca Wright that Haley's Aunt Penny had been rushed to the hospital. Moved by compassion, he'd called his favorite florist and had flowers delivered to the woman's hospital room.

In the few moments of casual conversation that they'd had, Haley had captivated him. It was more than just her womanly curves. Sure, she was beautiful and accomplished, but he met attractive, successful women every day. It was the emotion he'd seen on her face when she'd found out her aunt was ill that had touched him. Ashton was surrounded by people whose emotions were buried deep inside. He, himself, was a master at concealing his feelings.

He didn't feel comfortable opening up to anyone. Not even the people he loved most. Sadly, the accident had changed everything.

The words froze in his brain. *The accident.* Bitter memories darkened his mind. No one ever talked about it. Ashton thought about his college days. At Nilson University, he'd dated Mia Landers, a scholarship student who had had a crush on him for several years. His parents didn't like Mia, but he figured they'd come around. His father suggested that Ashton was dating Mia as a form of delayed adolescent rebellion, and his mother, Joan, labeled Mia "common" and "a nobody." But Ashton had continued dating her. He hadn't cared what they thought. It was his life.

The day Ashton told his parents he'd proposed to Mia,

all hell had broken loose at the Rollins estate. His father claimed Mia didn't belong in their world, wasn't welcome, and had no place in their family. Enraged, Ashton had stood his ground, arguing that if they took the time to get to know her, instead of judging her, they'd love her as much as he did. Tragically, Ashton had never had the opportunity to prove what an incredible woman his fiancée was.

Pain stabbed Ashton's heart, and his vision blurred. Shortly after graduation, he and Mia were in a car accident that had proved fatal for her. He'd woken up in the hospital with no memory of the accident, but Mia had died at the scene. Alexander said authorities believed Mia must have been drinking and she'd lost control of her car. The police report made no sense to Ashton. Mia was not a drinker. And when they were together, he always drove, even if it was her car. "Mia was driving," Alexander had said firmly. "Be thankful. If you were driving, you could have been charged with manslaughter."

Weeks later, Ashton had received devastating news. The autopsy report claimed there were drugs in Mia's system. His family had managed to keep the information out of the press, but that was the least of Ashton's problems. He'd lost the love of his life, and hated his father's cold, callous attitude about the accident. He'd attended Mia's funeral in a wheelchair, in a haze of grief and confusion, and had nightmares about the accident for several months.

Once his physical injuries healed, he'd been worried about his future. Would people blame him for Mia's death? Would he lose his acceptance to business school? Would his reputation be destroyed? His parents had instructed him not to speak of the incident to people outside of the family. If there was gossip and speculation about what had caused the mishap, Ashton wasn't privy to it. To this day, more than ten years after Mia's death, the incident was never spoken of in the Rollins household. Occasionally, he still dreamt about it but in his waking hours, he sometimes wondered if the accident had really happened. If he'd ever even had a fiancée.

Taking off his aviator sunglasses, Ashton rubbed at his eyes. Since the car accident, he'd toed the line where his family was concerned. He'd gotten his Ivy League MBA and gone to work at Rollins Aeronautics. He only dated women his parents considered "appropriate." But not once had he fallen in love. He continued to feel guilty about Mia's death, though everyone told him it wasn't his fault. Why hadn't he realized she was under the influence? Why had he let her get behind the wheel? If he had been driving, the accident could have been avoided, and he'd be married now, not heartbroken and alone.

Again, Haley Adams barged into his thoughts. For the first time in years, Ashton was open to having a girlfriend, and the only person on his radar was the charity CEO.

Curious how Haley was doing, Ashton retrieved his cell phone from his jacket pocket and called her. On a whim, he'd phoned Haley a couple times from Frankfurt, but every time he called she was unavailable. Today, though, he was determined to finally connect with her.

"Good morning. The Aunt Penny Foundation," chirped a female voice. "This is Stacy speaking. How may I help you?"

"Hello. Can I please speak to Ms. Haley Adams?"

"I'm sorry, sir, but she's in a meeting. Would you like to leave a message?"

No, I want you to put her on the phone so I can ask her out! Frustrated, Ashton hung up and chucked his cell on the seat. Damn, why was it so hard to get Haley on the line? She was the CEO of a charity organization, for goodness' sake, not the leader of the free world!

And he was a Rollins. Why was he sitting there pouting? He sat up, straightening his shoulders. He didn't wait for things to happen. He made things happen.

Imbued with confidence, a plan taking shape in his mind, he pressed the intercom button.

"Yes, Mr. Rollins?" the driver asked. "How may I be of assistance?"

"Take me to The Aunt Penny Foundation, and step on it. It's important."

"Very well, sir. Not a problem. I'll have you there quick, fast and in a hurry!"

The driver punched the gas, sending the limousine flying down Brickell Avenue.

Pleased, Ashton adjusted his pin-striped tie. This time when he saw Haley, things would be different. The thought—and the images of the curvy, dark-skinned beauty—excited him.

Twenty minutes later, the limousine stopped in front of a brown brick building, and Ashton stepped out. "Thanks. Hang tight. I'll be back in ten minutes."

Modern and clean, the reception area was decorated with children's artwork, bamboo plants, brown leather furniture and brass lamps. Approaching the front desk, he buttoned his suit jacket and took off his sunglasses.

"Good morning," greeted the receptionist at the mahogany desk. "Welcome to The Aunt Penny Foundation. How may I help you?"

Licking his lips, Ashton peered down the hallway, hoping to catch a glimpse of her. He was a great judge of character, and something told him Haley Adams was special. Someone he could trust. More than just a pretty face and a sexy body. Ashton wanted to know if their connection was real, or a figment of his imagination, and there was only one way to find out. "I'm Ashton Rollins, president of Prescott George, and I'm here to see Ms. Haley Adams."

Frowning, worry lines wrinkling her brow, she consulted her appointment book. "One moment, please," she chirped, raising an index finger in the air.

She snatched the phone off the cradle, pressed 0 and spoke in a low, hushed voice to the person on the line. Ashton couldn't hear what she was saying, but it didn't matter. He wasn't leaving until he saw Haley.

"Ms. Adams will see you now." The receptionist sprang to her feet. "Right this way, Mr. Rollins."

Following her down the corridor, Ashton heard telephones ringing, the distant sound of laughter and the familiar chug of a photocopier. Inspirational quotes were painted on the deep blue walls, words of encouragement and hope, and reading them lifted his spirits. Coming to The Aunt Penny Foundation was a bold move, one Ashton was confident would pay off. The air smelled of peppermint and perfume, a fragrant aroma that made him think of Haley, and he suspected she was nearby.

Stopping at the end of the hallway, the receptionist gestured to the open door to her left.

Nodding his thanks, Ashton entered the bright, sun-drenched office. And there, standing behind the executive desk in a fitted cardigan, white V-neck dress and pearls was Haley Adams. His crush. The object of his affection. The woman who'd starred in his dreams last night—and the night before last. The urge to touch her was overwhelming, but since he was a gentleman and not a sex-crazed teenager, he stayed put and buried his hands inside his pockets.

Staring at her, Ashton admired her creamy skin, slender nose, glossy red lips and high cheekbones. Her stylish auburn bob grazed her shoulders, and the short, thick bangs complemented her oval face, drawing attention to her big brown eyes.

"Welcome to The Aunt Penny Foundation, Mr. Rollins. What can I do for you?"

Ashton choked down a laugh. Her mouth said, "Welcome," but her cold, rigid stance said, "Get out and don't come back!" Fidgeting with her fingers, she shifted and shuffled her feet, causing Ashton to remember the last time he'd done The Electric Slide. It was at a friend's wedding reception months earlier, and when his date—an uptight scientist from Coral Gables—had complained the song was corny, he'd hit the dance floor alone.

"It's great to see you again, Haley. How is Aunt Penny doing?"

Eyes wide, she stared at him as if he'd just asked for her hand in marriage.

"I hope she's feeling better," he added, "and is finally out of the hospital."

"Yes, she is. Thanks for asking."

Noting the photographs on the mauve walls—pictures of Haley at a ribbon-cutting ceremony, posing with a group of college graduates, shaking hands with the mayor—Ashton walked further into the small, cramped space. Wholly feminine, it had a hot pink corkboard, vases overflowing with sunflowers, a colorful area rug and glass shelves lined with business management books, postcards and potted candles. "Ms. Wright did an outstanding job with her presentation for Prescott George, but I have some questions about The Aunt Penny Foundation that I'm hoping you can answer."

"Absolutely," she said, speaking in a breathless tone. "I'm free now."

Haley gestured to the armchair in front of her desk, but Ashton didn't move.

"Sorry, but I can't stay." For effect, he glanced at his

gold wrist watch and slowly shook his head, as if he was profoundly disappointed. "I'm pressed for time, but perhaps you can come to my Fisher Island estate tonight at six o'clock. We can talk then."

"Your estate?" Her voice rose an octave. "Tonight?"

"Yes, my estate. Is that a problem?"

Panic flickered across her face, but she fervently shook her head. "No, not at all."

"Great. I'll leave my address and cell number with your receptionist on my way out."

"Thank you, Mr. Rollins. I look forward to seeing you later."

"Call me Ashton. All of my friends do, and I have a feeling we'll be buddies in no time."

Her face lit up. "I'd like that."

That makes two of us, he thought. *Getting to know you better is priority number one.*

A raw, primal hunger he'd never experienced surged through his body. Ashton wanted to take Haley in his arms for a kiss, but he didn't. Couldn't. Not until he knew more about her. Did she have a boyfriend? Several? Was she attracted to him, too, or was he fooling himself? He hoped it wasn't the latter.

"Enjoy the rest of your day," he said, putting on his sunglasses. "Don't work too hard."

"Likewise, Mr. President."

Amused at her joke, Ashton chuckled. "Funny, successful *and* gorgeous? What a winning combination. *You* should be my first lady."

Her laughter tickled his ears, and the jovial expression on her face made him feel proud, as if he'd hit a hole in one on a golf course. They stared at each other, and her gaze was so strong and intense Ashton couldn't move. Couldn't catch his breath. He didn't like losing control and hated feeling weak, powerless. He turned away from her to break the spell.

"I better get back to work, or I'll never make it out of here on time." Plopping down on her zebra-print chair, she crossed her legs and picked up the pen on her desk calendar. "Thanks for stopping by, Ashton. I'll see you at six."

I can't wait.

He'd done it. Asked out the sexiest, most captivating woman he'd ever met, and Ashton hoped tonight would be the first of many dates. Anxious to return to his estate to begin making preparations for their romantic dinner, he strode out the door with a Cheshire-cat grin, confident it would be a night he'd never forget.

An hour after leaving The Aunt Penny Foundation, Ashton entered the entryway of his eight-bedroom estate. Dropping his house keys in the porcelain bowl on the marble table, he kicked off his shoes and loosened the knot in his Burberry tie. It was good to be home, he thought, his gaze circling the foyer. He'd lived at the estate for years, but he still loved everything about the mansion—the vaulted ceilings and stone columns, the Mediterranean architecture, the plush furniture and the lush palm trees and foliage visible from every window. His parents lived next door, and although there was a sprawling lawn between the two properties, like it or not, his parents dropped by every day—sometimes twice.

"Where have you been? Your plane landed hours ago."

Ashton cranked his head to the right, seeing his father standing there in the doorway to the den. *"Mi casa es su casa,"* he joked, right before he added, "Dad, it's good to see you."

"What took you so long to get home?" Alexander inquired. "I've been waiting for you."

Thoughts of Haley flooded his mind, and his temperature rose. "I had a stop to make."

"We need to talk. It's important."

"Dad, don't worry, my trip was fine. I made a lot of valuable business contacts at the Aerospace Expo and I plan to return to Germany later this year for Oktoberfest. Not only is it a great networking opportunity, it's—"

"That's not why I'm here. Trouble's brewing within the Moguls." Taking a puff of his cigar, his father sat down in a leather armchair. "Joshua DeLong is plotting to unseat you."

Ashton shrugged. "Big deal. More power to him."

"That's it? That's all you have to say?"

"Dad, I have bigger things to worry about than who's doing what in Prescott George. I have a company to run, an anniversary party to plan…"

And a woman to seduce, he thought, but didn't say for fear his dad would blab to his mom. The last thing Ashton wanted was Joan dropping by to grill him about Haley.

"I don't think you understand the gravity of the situation," Alexander said, his eyes narrowed and his tone clipped. "You have to act now, before it's too late."

Hearing his cell phone buzz, Alexander checked the screen. A grim expression darkened his face. Surging to his feet, he put his cell to his ear and strode out of the room. As his father brushed past him and marched down the hall, Ashton overheard him say, "What did you find out? Who does DeLong have in his back pocket, and what do we have to do to regain the upper hand?"

Perplexed, Ashton stroked his jaw. Was he missing something? Was there more to the story? He couldn't understand why his dad was so unnerved by the rumors—and why he'd come over to tell him about it in person. The members of Prescott George would never allow an interloper like Joshua DeLong to take over, and Ashton had better things to do with his time than stress about what the smug corporate raider was up to. Furthermore, Ashton was a strong leader who had the unwavering support of his members, and there was nothing Joshua could do about it.

Clearing his mind of every troubling thought, Ashton strode down the hallway, whistling a tune. After he spoke to his chef and touched base with his assistant, he was going to the barber shop. He had to look his best for Haley. Ashton couldn't remember the last time he'd been this excited about someone, and sensed it was going to be a night to remember. He only hoped his father didn't make another unexpected visit and ruin his date.

Chapter 2

Haley sat inside her red, two-door coupe, which was parked on the Rollinses' winding, cobblestone driveway, giving herself a pep talk. Her hands were damp with sweat, shaking so hard she couldn't open the car door, and butterflies fluttered inside her stomach.

"I can do this. I can do this," Haley chanted, drawing strength from her words. "I have nothing to be afraid of. It doesn't matter that Ashton has piercing brown eyes, a panty-wetting voice and a muscled physique. It's just a business dinner. No big deal."

Then why are your knees knocking together? her inner voice asked.

Dismissing the question, Haley told herself she had nothing to worry about. Besides, it was too late to change her mind. If she left now it would ruin everything. Add to that, getting to Fisher Island had been an exhausting ordeal, and she was starving. After getting her name cleared by security and ferrying her car across Biscayne Bay, she'd driven the ten miles to Ashton's opulent neighborhood. Home to celebrities, dignitaries and international businessmen, Fisher Island was remote, exclusive and elegant. She felt out of place driving past the custom-built mansions in her second-hand car. A tropical oasis with breathtaking scenery, Mediterranean architecture and luxury yachts, the island was described as "the playground of the rich." The Rollinses were the richest of the rich, and Haley hoped she didn't say or do anything to screw up her business meeting.

Opening the visor, Haley checked her hair and makeup for the umpteenth time. Wanting to look professional, she'd paired a canary-yellow sundress with a fitted cardigan, gold accessories and wedge sandals. She'd hastily added a touch of mascara and some lip gloss before heading out her condo door.

Haley took a deep breath. Enough stalling. Time to get the show on the road. The Aunt Penny Foundation was counting on her to secure the support of the Millionaire Moguls, and nothing was going to stop her. Not even her frazzled nerves.

The front door of the mansion swung open and Ashton appeared, instantly seizing her attention. Peering out of the windshield, Haley leaned forward in her seat. Tall, with dark skin, close-cropped hair and a neatly trimmed mustache and goatee, Ashton Rollins had a face made for movies and a body made for sin. Dressed in a blue button-down shirt, belted shorts and sandals, not only did he look handsome he exuded confidence and masculinity. There wasn't a woman alive who wouldn't find Ashton Rollins sexy, and seeing him again caused her pulse to soar and her heart to race. He was staring right at her. Watching her every move.

Grabbing her clutch purse off the passenger seat, Haley stepped out of the car, ready to meet the hottie COO with the thousand-watt smile. He was a one-night stand waiting to happen, and as he jogged down the steps goose bumps pricked her skin. Haley didn't know if she was sweating profusely because of the heat or because Ashton was headed her way, but she suspected it was the latter. He made her nervous, unsure of herself, and keeping her wits during dinner was going to be harder than riding a bicycle backwards in six-inch heels.

"Welcome to Fisher Island." Leaning in close, he kissed her cheek. "It's great to see you again, Haley."

"Thank you. It's a pleasure to be here. Your home is stunning."

"I have dinner waiting for us poolside. Do you like soul food?"

Haley smiled. "Of course I do. Doesn't everyone?"

Resting a hand on her lower back, Ashton guided her along the stone pathway that led to the rear of the mansion. "If you'd like, after dinner I can give you a tour of the estate..."

Wow, this is what heaven must look like, Haley thought, admiring the expansive grounds. The property was attractive and serene, and everything in the outdoor living room was state-of-the-art and designer quality. A wrought-iron table covered with fine china, bronze candelabra and a glass vase filled with sunflowers was beside the Olympic-size pool. The air smelled of spices, the savory aromas from the outdoor kitchen carrying on the breeze, and jazz played on the stereo system. Haley couldn't wait to tell Aunt Penny about the Rollins estate; she knew the eighty-eight-year-old senior would love hearing about her business dinner.

Ashton pulled out a chair at the table, and Haley thanked him. Taking a seat, she noticed a heavyset black woman with auburn braids emerge from the house carrying a gold serving tray in one hand and a pitcher in the other.

"Haley, this is my personal chef and surrogate mom, Ms. Edith."

"It's nice to meet you," Haley said, licking her lips. "Something smells delicious."

Wearing a proud smile, Ms. Edith set two bowls down on the table and filled their water glasses to the brim. "I'll be back shortly with the second course, so eat up before your soup gets cold."

"Ms. Edith don't play," Ashton whispered. "We'd better do as we're told, or we won't get dessert. I don't know about you but I *live* for peach cobbler."

Giggling, Haley stirred the thick, orange soup. It tasted so good she finished it within seconds.

"*Someone's* hungry," he teased, his eyes bright with mischief. "Would you like more?"

"No, I'm pacing myself. I have to save room for the next course, because it's obvious Ms. Edith's an exceptional cook, and I want to try everything she made tonight."

"How do you know I didn't make the soup?"

Hayley scoffed. "You? Cook? I bet you can't even boil water."

"You're right, I can't, but I did a hell of a job setting the table!"

They shared a laugh, and Haley realized she'd been stressed out for nothing. Despite his wealth and social status, Ashton wasn't a smug, stuck-up rich boy. He was personable and laid-back, easy to talk to, and cracked more jokes than a comedian on Comedy Central.

"We should discuss The Aunt Penny Foundation," she said, curious why he'd invited her to his estate. "What's on your mind?"

"Tell me how you got involved with the organization."

His question confused her. Frowning, she cocked her head to the right. Hadn't he read the dossier Becca had submitted in May about the foundation? Hadn't he paid attention during her colleague's presentation? Telling herself it didn't matter, Haley opened up to him about her family background and her fifteen-year relationship with Penny Washington. "When I was a kid, my parents worked several jobs, and our neighbor, Ms. Penny, took pity on me because I was home alone a lot. She never married and had no children of her own, and she looked out for me," she explained, as happy memories filled her mind. "If not for Aunt Penny's kindness and generosity I never would have been able to afford to go to university."

"She sounds like an incredible person. You're lucky to have her."

"I know, that's why I came up with the idea for a nonprofit organization that would give other talented, gifted youth from the inner city an Aunt Penny of their own..."

Ms. Edith returned, and Haley waited as the cook cleared the empty bowls, put down plates of cornbread salad and promptly left. Remembering the last time she'd had soul food made her heart sad. She'd joined her ex-boyfriend and his loved ones to celebrate his dad's seventieth birthday. It felt bittersweet to think about the fun, gregarious Argentinian family she'd come to love as her own. Haley wanted to be with someone who was loyal and supportive, who wouldn't try to change her or control her—and even though her ex had turned out to be Mr. Wrong, she still missed his family. She hadn't dated anyone since their breakup last year, but Haley was tired of being single, and wanted one special man in her life.

"Do you like your job?"

His question broke into her thoughts. "I love it. It's the best job I've ever had."

"How long have you been CEO?"

"For three years, and even though the foundation has faced some trying times in recent months, there's nowhere else I'd rather work. I have a dedicated, committed team, and incredible sponsors in my corner as well."

"Tell me more about the services The Aunt Penny Foundation provides." Ashton reached for his glass and took a drink.

"We provide counselling, tutoring in all subject areas, and our job preparation classes offer coaching, help with résumés, and even mock interviews."

Ashton raised an eyebrow. Haley could tell that he was impressed with the work they were doing at The Aunt Penny Foundation.

"That's terrific, Haley. It sounds like you and your staff are doing fantastic work in the community."

Touched by his words, she smiled in response. "Thanks, Ashton. We're trying our best."

"How many scholarships are awarded each year, and what criteria are used to select the recipients?"

"Every year, we receive dozens of scholarship applications, and incredible personal essays, but unfortunately we can only award five scholarships. We select recipients in financial need with high academic achievement, who have volunteered for a minimum of one year."

"I'm thrilled Prescott George is partnering with The Aunt Penny Foundation this year. It's the smartest thing we've ever done, and I look forward to learning more about you, and your brilliant students..."

Haley listened in awe as he spoke. She met with businessmen on a regular basis on behalf of the foundation, but she'd never met anyone like Ashton. Unlike the hedge fund manager she'd had brunch with yesterday, he didn't drone on and on about his high-profile job, or his staggering wealth.

Instead, he was gracious and kind. A part of her couldn't help wondering if he'd be so nice to her if he knew her BFF, Becca, was engaged to his nemesis, Joshua DeLong. That afternoon, she'd bumped into the happy couple as they were leaving the foundation's offices for lunch, and when Haley mentioned she was having dinner with Ashton that evening Joshua had scowled.

His words replayed in her mind, drowning out the BB King song playing on the stereo. *Be careful. Don't fall under Ashton's spell. He's not who you think he is.*

From her talks with Becca, Haley knew that there was no love lost between the two men, and that Joshua was planning to challenge Ashton in the upcoming election for president of Prescott George. The corporate raider had claimed Ashton was trouble, a bad seed, but Haley took his admonitions with a grain of salt. The Rollinses were an old, respected Miami family, and she doubted Ashton had ever done anything sinister or illegal. Besides, he was throwing his support behind The Aunt Penny Foundation, and that was good enough for her.

"I'd love to hear more about your family's company," Haley said, tired of hearing herself talk. "How long has Rollins Aeronautics been in business, and who founded it?"

"My grandfather George and his partner, Prescott Owens, founded the company in 1938. Five years later, they became the first black millionaires in Florida. Rollins Aeronautics has stayed profitable through the generations. I run the day-to-day operations of the company, and when my father retires next year I'll assume his duties as CEO."

Ms. Edith reappeared, carrying plates topped with lamb chops, collard greens, shrimp-fried rice and okra. Haley's mouth watered at the sight of the main course, but she waited until Ashton was finished eating his salad before tasting her entrée.

While they ate, they had a spirited discussion about the day's news stories. Haley was intrigued by Ashton. Couldn't help it. It wasn't every day she met a man of his caliber, who shared her likes and interests. Having dinner with him was turning out to be the best part of her day.

Sipping her drink, she admired the tranquil surroundings. The views of the water were as spectacular as the food. Each course was flavorful and delicious, and by the time Ms. Edith brought out dessert Haley was so full she couldn't move. The meal got an A for presentation and an A+ for taste, but what she enjoyed most was getting to know her handsome host better.

"What would I do if I wasn't working at the foundation?" Repeating the question posed by Ashton seconds earlier, Haley gave it some serious thought. "If I wasn't CEO of The Aunt Penny Foundation I'd probably work at a hardware store."

Ashton frowned. "A hardware store? Why?"

"Because I love building things," she explained, unable to hide her excitement. "I attend free workshops at Home Depot several times a month to improve my skills, and last week my instructor said my birdhouse was the best one in the class."

"You strike me as the type who likes to bake, not swing a hammer."

"Growing up, I was a tomboy. I rode dirt bikes, played video games and never left home without my beloved Firebirds baseball cap."

"And now?"

"I still enjoy playing sports, but I've definitely embraced my feminine side." She joked, "Being a woman is great! I can change my look whenever the mood strikes and my shoe collection would make Jimmy Choo jealous!"

"You're a talented young woman who's destined to do

great things in the nonprofit sector, *and* at Home Depot." Ashton smiled. "Your boyfriend must be very proud of you."

For the second time in minutes, her mind ran to her ex-boyfriend, Federico Tevez. A year ago they'd been making plans for the future, but now their relationship was over, nothing but a distant memory. Their breakup had been painful, but for the best. He'd moved to Washington, DC, as planned—without her—and every time someone mentioned the nation's capital, Haley wondered what could have been. On paper, they were a perfect match. He was a trained chef with big dreams and traditional values, but—

Stop dwelling on the past, Haley told herself, breaking free of her thoughts. *He wasn't the right man for you. You have to accept that and move on. He's not coming back.*

"I don't have a boyfriend," she said quietly. "I'm single."

"So am I. It's amazing how much we have in common."

His husky voice was dreamy, and when their eyes met, her mind went blank. It felt good being with a suave, charming man who smelled divine and showered her with compliments, and Haley wanted to spend the rest of the night hanging out with him.

"Can I ask you something?"

Curious, Haley nodded her head. "Sure, Ashton, what is it?"

"Why are you single?"

"Why are *you*?" she quipped.

A mischievous expression covered his face. "I asked first."

"I haven't met the right person yet. You?"

"Yesterday, I would have said the same thing, but I've recently had a change of heart. I'm interested in a beautiful, charity CEO, but I don't want to scare her off by revealing my true feelings." Ashton winked. "I'm pacing myself. It's only our first date."

Their eyes lined up.

"I had fun tonight," he said, "and I'd love to see you again."

Haley moistened her lips with her tongue. "To discuss The Aunt Penny Foundation?"

"No," he said calmly. "To wine you and dine you."

Ashton brushed his fingers against hers, and a moan rose in her throat.

Needing a moment to gather her thoughts, Haley sipped her water.

"Have you ever been to the Rooftop Bar?" he asked her. "It's the most popular restaurant-lounge in the city, and everything on the menu is exquisite."

You're exquisite, she thought, staring at his lips, wishing they were pressed hard against hers. "No, not yet. I've heard about it, but I haven't had an opportunity to check it out."

"I'll pick you up on Friday night at seven o'clock," he said with a broad grin, his tone matter-of-fact. "Wear comfortable shoes. We're going to be doing a lot of dancing."

"Ashton, I'm sorry, but I have other plans tomorrow night."

The smile slid off his face. "Do you have a date?"

"Yeah, a date at the Miami Soup Kitchen. Fun times!" Haley laughed. "I volunteer twice a week, and if I'm not there to make my seafood gumbo the regulars will complain."

"Need some help?"

"But you don't cook."

"Yeah," Ashton conceded. "But I can chop vegetables with the best of them."

"Then we'd love to have you."

"Great. I look forward to seeing you again on Friday night."

"Wear comfortable shoes," she teased, gesturing under

the table at his designer sandals. "Those aren't going to cut it. You're going to be on your feet all night, so runners are your best bet."

"Got it," Ashton said. "How did you get involved with the soup kitchen?"

Heat warmed her skin. Normally, Haley wasn't afraid to share her story, but she didn't want Ashton to judge her, and had second thoughts about opening up to him about her childhood. "Despite my parents both working two jobs, there was never enough food at home, so we'd eat at local soup kitchens a few times a week," she explained. "I started volunteering when I was in high school, and now I'm there so much it's like my second home."

A sympathetic expression covered his face, and Haley wished she'd kept her big mouth shut. Wished she'd lied. She didn't want Ashton's pity; she'd made it, built a life she was proud of. Thanks to Aunt Penny, she was an inner-city success story, and she'd never, ever forget where she came from.

"Please give my regards to Ms. Edith," she said, resting her utensils on her empty plate. "Dinner was amazing, especially her peach cobbler."

Ashton stood, came around the table and helped Haley out of her chair. "I'm glad you liked it. Next time you come over I'll see to it that she makes another one."

Next time? Her mouth watered, and her heart danced inside her chest.

"This was nice, Ashton. Thank you for a lovely evening—"

"You can't leave. I haven't given you a tour of the estate yet. It's not to be missed."

"Okay, one short tour, but then I have to go. It's *way* past my bedtime."

"If you're tired you can stay here. I have eight bedrooms and a huge guest cottage."

"I bet you say that to all the charity CEOs you have over for dinner."

Winking, he slid an arm around her waist. "No, beautiful, just you."

Chapter 3

Ashton wondered what Haley was thinking, wished he could read her mind and dissect her thoughts. Desire simmered below the surface, filling the air with its intoxicating fragrance. Stunning, with impeccable manners and a wicked sense of humor, Haley was hard to resist. All Ashton could think about was kissing her, ravishing her mouth with his. He found her delightful, genuine and sweet, and he didn't want her to leave. To prolong their time together, Ashton walked slowly along the winding pathway, stopping to point out the exotic fish in the man-made lake, the guest cottage and the outdoor basketball court.

"Next time you come over bring your workout gear. We'll play a game of one-on-one."

"Just say when." Haley grinned. "Don't worry. I'll take it easy on you."

"I've been playing basketball since I was in diapers. You don't stand a chance."

"Ha, ha, ha," she quipped, her tone full of sarcasm.

"You're hilarious! We'll see who gets the last laugh when I cream you on your own court!"

Ashton cracked up. Haley looked pleased with herself, as if she'd hit a three-point shot from half-court, and the jovial expression on her face made her eyes twinkle.

"I don't care how good you think your game is, Haley. You're going down."

"Your mama!"

Tossing his head back, Ashton erupted in laughter. He'd dated women from all walks of life, who always said and did the right thing, but he found her personality refreshing. Haley told it like it was, and their verbal sparring was a turn-on, putting him in a playful mood.

"This is a huge house for one person." Haley stared up at him, shielding her eyes from the setting sun with her hands. Hands he wished were on his body, stroking his—

"Do you live with your parents?"

"Hell no!" Ashton said, shivering at the thought. "They live next door."

As they strolled around the property, every other word out of Haley's mouth was "Wow," "Incredible," or "Awesome." She listened as he talked about the mansion and asked him numerous questions. How many years did it take to build the estate? Did he have live-in staff? Did he entertain regularly? It amused him to see her reaction to his house, to hear her shriek when something shocked her—like the size of his home gym—and Ashton wondered if Haley was vocal in the bedroom, too.

"This room is bigger than my entire condo," she said, glancing around the space, her eyes wide with wonder. "I'd kill to have a home gym like this."

The air-conditioned room was filled with state-of-the-art exercise equipment. Autographed posters of famous athletes hung on the vibrant blue walls, and the walk-in fridge at the rear of the room was stocked with healthy snacks and cold drinks. It was Ashton's favorite room in the house, and whenever he had a bad day or argued with his dad, he'd head straight to the gym and exercise until he was in a better frame of mind.

"I feel like I'm in a museum. I'm going to need a map to find my way out of here!"

"Don't worry. I'll escort you to your car when you're ready to go."

Frowning, Haley pointed at the red floor mat in front of the window. "You do yoga?"

"Of course." Ashton grinned. "I'm more than just a pretty face, you know."

"No offense, but I don't know any guys who do yoga. How did you start?"

His former fiancée had begged him to attend her drop-in class and he hadn't wanted to disappoint her. But he didn't share that information with Haley. Not yet. It was too soon. Talking about Mia's death would upset him, and Ashton didn't want to ruin his date by getting emotional.

"I took a class my sophomore year of college," he said instead, "and I've been hooked ever since."

"No way! I never would have guessed it. You strike me as the type who likes to do extreme sports, not the downward dog. Do your friends give you a hard time for doing yoga?"

"Yeah, but once I told them Dwayne 'The Rock' Johnson, David Beckham and LeBron James swear by it, they quit teasing me. Yoga helps me focus and improves my mental toughness, and I wouldn't be the man I am without it."

"I've never tried it, but it looks hard, and I don't want to hurt myself."

"You won't," he assured her, hoping to put her fears at

ease. "If you'd like, I can schedule a private session with my trainer next week so you can see the physical and mental benefits for yourself. You know what they say, a couple who does yoga together stays together."

Shaking her head, Haley waved her hands in front of her face. "I better not. My best friend and I tried a Pilates class last month, and I was so sore the next day I couldn't move."

"And you think you can beat *me* in basketball? Keep dreaming."

"Just watch me," she quipped, all smiles. "I have skills you can't even imagine."

Were they still talking about basketball? Ashton wondered, wetting his lips with his tongue. Her soft, sultry tone tickled his eardrums, and her mischievous grin stole his breath. *What the hell?* Ashton thought, plucking at his shirt to cool down his suddenly overheated body. *I'm supposed to be in control, not her!*

Ashton couldn't stop staring at her. Haley looked prim and proper in her cardigan, like a preschool teacher on picture day, but she had an edge, a side to her he wanted to get to know better. And he would. Tonight. After they toured his estate.

Exiting the room, his hand placed firmly on her lower back, Ashton led her down the hallway to the den. They discussed the décor, the African-themed paintings and the souvenirs he'd purchased during his overseas travels, which were prominently displayed on the glass shelves.

"Do you travel a lot for work?"

Ashton nodded. "Yes. As a matter of fact, I returned from Frankfurt this morning."

"I'm so jealous. I wish I could travel more, but the foundation keeps me very busy."

"I know how you feel. As COO, it's my job to build and

promote Rollins Aeronautics, and this month alone, I'll be in Seattle, Orlando and Venezuela."

A concerned expression touched her delicate features. "Aren't you worried about your safety? Yesterday I read about the food shortages and increased crime in Maracaibo, and even locals are scared to venture out at night."

"All the more reason I should attend the conference," he said in a confident tone of voice. "The Venezuelan economy could use a boost, and in spite of the media reports it remains one of my favorite countries in the world. It has spectacular landscapes, some of the kindest, friendliest people you'll ever meet and the best food you've ever tasted."

"And it doesn't hurt that Venezuelan women are stunning," she pointed out.

"I never noticed."

"Right. Next you're going to tell me you've never been to a strip club!"

"I haven't. It's not my speed. I'd rather do yoga or play chess."

Haley studied the framed pictures along the walls. "Is there anywhere you haven't been yet that you're dying to travel to?"

"Ibiza." A grin overwhelmed Ashton's mouth. "We'll go there for our honeymoon."

Nodding, she returned his smile. "Deal. Give me the wedding of my dreams, and I'll travel the world with you!"

I love the sound of that, he thought, gazing down at her pretty face.

Continuing the tour, they walked through the main house and into the great room. They talked about growing up in Miami, their university days and their respective jobs. Haley was passionate about The Aunt Penny Foundation and giving back to her community, and Ashton enjoyed learning more about her hobbies and interests. Talking and cracking jokes, they moved from one topic to the next without missing a beat.

"What's your most prized possession?" Haley asked, admiring the glass sculptures on the end tables.

"That's easy. My car collection."

Ashton heard his cell phone ring inside his back pocket, knew from the ringtone it was his mother and decided to let the call go to voice mail. If he answered and mentioned he was on a date, she'd race over, and Ashton wasn't ready to introduce Haley to Joan. Not after one date. For now, he wanted to keep their relationship under wraps.

"Do you collect antique cars and motorcycles?"

"Why tell you when I can show you?"

Taking her hand, he led her down the corridor and into the garage, and flipped on the lights. It was a car aficionado's paradise, filled with several luxury vehicles.

"Wow, what a beauty." Haley peered inside the window of the Porsche and Ashton envisioned himself making love to her, right then and there, on the hood of his beloved sports car. But he wouldn't. Not tonight. Even though his body had other ideas, he was going to be on his best behavior and prove to her—and himself—that he could be a perfect gentleman.

"I've always wanted a Porsche, but it's *way* out of my tax bracket."

Ashton studied her closely. He saw the envy in her eyes, the interest and curiosity. To impress her, he grabbed the key fob off the silver wall hook and dropped it in her palm. "Hop in," he said, opening the driver's side door. "Let's take it for a spin."

"I—I—I can't drive your car." Haley pushed the keys back into his hands.

Confused by her reaction, Ashton frowned. "Why not?"

"Because it costs more than I make in a year. I'd feel funny driving it."

"Don't worry," he said, giving her a one-arm hug. Ashton liked touching her,, and didn't want to let her go. She smelled of summer fruit, causing his mouth to water, and she fit perfectly in his arms. "Nothing's going to happen. There's not much traffic on Fisher Island. Most residents use golf carts to get around, not cars."

Haley backed away from the Porsche, and Ashton grabbed her hand. Surprise flashed in her eyes, but he didn't release his hold. His first thought was to kiss her, but since he didn't want to push his luck he escorted her to the passenger-side door and opened it.

"No problem. I'll drive." To lighten the mood and make her feel at ease, he said, "We can stop at Pastries and More for a snack. It's the most popular dessert shop on the island, and their cotton candy ice cream is the best thing I've ever tasted."

Haley put on her seat belt. "Then what are we waiting for? Let's go!"

Deciding to give her a tour of the island first, Ashton pulled out of the garage and drove cautiously down the driveway. In his rearview mirror, he spotted his mother standing on his doorstep and floored the gas. If he stopped, Joan would question Haley about everything under the sun—her education background, her career aspirations, her ten-year goals—and Ashton didn't want his mom to scare her off. Mindful of the neighbor's children playing hockey on the street, he slowed as he exited the security gate and waved at them.

"Do you have plans on Saturday?" he asked, glancing at her.

"No, not yet. I was thinking of going to Pensacola, to

surprise my mom, but she has to work, so I'll be home this weekend. Why? What are you up to?"

"I'm going to the Firebirds game, and I want you to come."

Seconds passed and Ashton feared Haley was going to turn him down, but she surprised him by cracking a joke.

"Only if you buy me lunch first," she said with a teasing smile.

"Deal, and I'll even throw in dessert."

"How can I turn down such a generous offer?"

Haley laughed, and Ashton knew he was making progress with her. He felt a connection to her, feelings he'd never experienced before, and he wanted to explore them further. Haley crossed her legs, and Ashton had to remind himself to drive, not lust. It was a challenge to keep his eyes on the road and off Haley's curves, but he forced himself to focus.

"This car drives like a dream," she said, running a hand along the side paneling.

Images of Mia flashed in Ashton's head. *I'm having déjà vu*, he thought, swallowing hard, willing the moment to pass. It didn't. His memories were clear, gripping, powerful. He remembered helping Mia into the passenger seat of his Maserati, and sliding in behind the wheel. Like he had moments earlier with Haley.

Sweat trickled down the back of his shirt. The images haunted him, flashing in his head, leaving Ashton dazed and confused. Feeling light-headed, he slammed on the brakes. He gripped the steering wheel and took a deep breath to slow his erratic heartbeat.

"Ashton, what's wrong? You're shaking."

"I'm fine."

"No, you're not. Talk to me. I want to help." Haley inclined her body toward his and rested a hand on his forearm. "What is it?"

Sadness and regret flooded Ashton's heart. He could tell by Haley's furrowed brow that she was confused by his odd behavior, but he wasn't ready to open up to her about his past. What could he say? *"Sorry, I just remembered driving with my dead girlfriend?"* Haley would run for the hills, and Ashton didn't want her to think he was crazy. Part of him felt stupid for inviting her to his estate in the first place, but another part of him was glad he'd made the first move.

"Let's go back to the house. We can talk there."

"What about the ice cream? You had your heart set on having the cotton candy flavor."

"I'll survive. Besides, I'm still full from dinner."

Haley stared at him with trusting, understanding eyes, as if to say everything would be okay, and although he'd promised himself he wouldn't make a move on her tonight, he leaned over and kissed her cheek. If Haley was surprised she didn't show it.

"Are you okay to drive," she asked him, "or do you want me to?"

"I'm good. Don't worry. I'll get you back to the estate in one piece."

Ashton merged into traffic, made a U-turn at Fisher Island Drive and cruised down the tree-lined street. He kept his eyes on the road, but sensing Haley was watching him, hummed with the song on the radio to prove everything was okay. Despite his reassurances, he could see she was worried about him and he felt like an ass for scaring her.

"We're back." Hoping to avoid a run-in with his mom, Ashton sped through the security gates and parked the Porsche in the garage. "Home sweet home."

"How are you feeling now?" Haley asked, her voice a whisper. "Any better?"

Projecting confidence, Ashton smiled and winked. "I'm

great. I'm having a good time with you and I'm looking forward to our date tomorrow night."

"Ashton, it's not a date. We're volunteering at the Miami Soup Kitchen together."

"Yeah, but after we finish up we're going to have drinks at the Rooftop Bar. They have a live reggae band on Friday nights, and they're one of the hottest acts in Miami."

Pop music played from inside Haley's handbag, and she scooped it up off the floor. "Ashton, do you mind if I take this call?"

"Not at all. Go ahead."

Putting the phone to her ear, Haley turned toward the passenger window and spoke in a soft, soothing voice. "Hello, Sienna, is everything okay?"

Watching her, Ashton could tell that something was wrong. The person on the line sounded hysterical, but he couldn't make out what the female caller was saying.

"Sweetie, stop crying. Everything's going to be fine. I promise." Haley took off her seat belt and threw open the passenger-side door. "Sienna, wait for me in front of your apartment building. I'm on my way. I'll be there as soon as I can."

Ashton jumped out of the Porsche and joined Haley on the driveway. Keys in hand, she marched toward her car, a frown on her lips, obviously deep in thought.

"You're leaving? Already? But it's only nine o'clock."

Haley dropped her cell inside her purse. "I'm sorry, but I have to go. It's an emergency."

"Is there anything I can do to help?"

Shaking her head, she slid behind the wheel. "Thank you for a wonderful evening," Haley said politely. "And for listening to my pitch about The Aunt Penny Foundation. The backing of the Millionaire Moguls means the world to me, and I want to thank you from the bottom of my heart for the support."

Before Ashton could respond, Haley put the car in Drive and sped down the drive.

Ashton wondered what his parents would think of her. She was a smart, educated woman, but she wasn't from a moneyed family. Questions loomed in his mind. Would his parents like her? Would they welcome her into the family with open arms? Or would his father give him a hard time for dating someone from humble beginnings?

Returning to the house, Ashton broke free of his thoughts. He was too old to cater to his mother and father. He wasn't a college student anymore. He was older now, wiser, capable of making his own decisions, and he didn't need anyone's approval to spend time with Haley Adams. He wanted to date her—planned to romance her every chance he got—and Ashton didn't give a damn what his bougie, uptight parents thought.

Chapter 4

"You're a sight for sore eyes," Becca quipped, her voice slicing through the noise in the staff room of The Aunt Penny Foundation. Grabbing the remote off one of the round, oak tables, she turned off the TV and hitched a hand to her hip. "How was your date with the president?"

Glancing up from the coffee machine, Haley rolled her eyes. It was 7:00 a.m. on Friday, much too early to be interrogated, but if she didn't respond Becca would hound her for the rest of the day. Soon, the room would be full of staff, and they'd have zero privacy, so Haley said, "His name is Ashton, and if you must know our business meeting went very well."

"Business meeting? Girl, please, it was a date and you know it."

Haley unzipped her nylon lunch bag and took out her breakfast. A creature of habit, she ate a banana and a whole wheat bagel every morning upon arriving at the office. She appreciated having a few quiet moments to herself to plan for the day and review her schedule, and hoped Becca didn't grill her about Ashton while she was eating. "Is that why you're here an hour early?" she asked, gesturing to the decorative wall clock above the door. "Because your nosy behind wants to find out what happened between me and Ashton?"

Becca giggled. "Heck yeah! I'm dying to hear all of the scandalous details."

Laughing, Haley cut her bagel in half, dropped it in the stainless-steel toaster and eyed Becca with fondness. Her best friend used to hide her long, lush curls in a bun, and her womanly curves under loose clothes, but once Becca met Joshua DeLong she'd revamped her look. Last month, they'd gone shopping at the most exclusive shops in Miami, and now Becca came to the office dressed like a participant in *America's Next Top Model.* Chic hairstyle, nails tastefully done, form-fitting outfits, designer accessories and shoes. Joshua had swept Becca off her feet, and everyone had noticed a big change in Becca, even Aunt Penny. Haley was thrilled for her best friend and hoped the happy couple had a long and prosperous marriage.

Not like me, she thought sadly. *I've never had a successful relationship.*

"I waited up for your call, and when I didn't hear from you I figured you gave Ashton the cookie and fell asleep at his gorgeous, to-die-for estate!"

"Wrong again."

Becca raised an eyebrow, and crossed her arms. Her belted shirtdress accentuated her slim body, and the indigo shade complemented her flawless brown skin. "You didn't spend the night at Ashton's place? Then why didn't I hear from you?"

"Sienna phoned me, crying hysterically, so I left Ashton's estate to go pick her up." Haley filled her pink, oversized mug with coffee and added a splash of cream. "I got in late, and since I knew you'd be sleeping, I figured we'd touch base today."

Concern covered her features. "What happened? Is Sienna okay?"

"No." Recalling her conversation with the high school sophomore last night as they sipped hot chocolate inside Haley's kitchen caused her good mood to fizzle. In the three years she'd been CEO at The Aunt Penny Foundation, she'd never seen a case as troubling as Sienna Larimore, but she was determined to help the shy, honor roll student. "Her mom's new boyfriend is saying and doing things to make her uncomfortable, and she's scared to be alone with him. Until I can arrange a meeting with her mom, she'll stay with me."

A frown crimped Becca's mouth.

"Don't look at me like that. I did what I thought was right."

"What happened to keeping your professional life and your personal life separate?"

"I know, I know, don't read me the riot act. It's just for a few days."

"You said that the last time, and Aaliyah and Faith both lived with you for months."

"What did you expect me to do? Sienna was upset and I didn't feel comfortable taking her back home," Haley explained, feeling the need to defend herself. "She's a sweet girl with incredible potential, and I'd never forgive myself if something bad happened to her."

Sighing, Becca shook her head. Haley couldn't tell if her bestie was on her side or not. In her heart, she knew she'd made the right decision and wished Becca couldn't give her a hard time about it. "Sienna said her mom's boyfriend teases her about her body and makes dirty jokes when they're alone. There was no way in hell I was taking her home to him."

"Creep," Becca spat, her tone full of disgust. "I wish I could be alone with him for five minutes. I'd put my self-defense training to good use."

"That makes two of us. I have a meeting with Sienna and her mom tomorrow, and I hope Ms. Larimore will take my concerns seriously."

"She better. Screw her boyfriend. She needs to do what's best for her daughter."

Becca bumped Haley aside with her hips, opened the fridge and grabbed a chocolate chip muffin, a can of orange juice and a cup of Greek yogurt from off the top shelf.

"You're trouble, you know that?" Haley said with a smile.

"Funny, Josh said the same thing last night when I handcuffed him to the bed!"

The women cracked up.

Becca sat down at the table. "Get over here," she ordered, pointing at the chair across from her. "I want a play-by-play of your date with Mr. President, and don't skip over the juicy parts. I want to hear it all."

Mug and plate in hand, Haley stared longingly at the staff room door. She wanted to make a break for it, to run full-speed down the hall and into her office, but reluctantly sat down. She was attracted to Ashton, but that was all it was—a silly, hopeless crush that wouldn't amount to anything—and she'd rather discuss work than her feelings for the sinfully handsome COO.

Over breakfast, Haley gave Becca the CliffsNotes version of her evening with Ashton, careful to leave out how delicious he smelled and how wonderful his touch had made her feel. "I thought Ashton was going to be smug, like some of the other wealthy executives I've met in recent months, but he's actually a really nice guy. Down-to-earth, chivalrous and genuine."

"I don't know, girl. Josh is a great judge of character, and he thinks Ashton's trouble."

"Of course he does. He's a corporate raider. He's suspicious of everyone!"

Becca laughed, and her dark brown curls tumbled around her face. "Good point, but..." Shaking her head, she trailed off speaking, and waved a hand absently in the air. "Forget it. I've said enough."

"No, go ahead, Becca. I want to hear what you have to say."

Several seconds passed before she spoke.

"Josh said there are things about Ashton people would be shocked to know. Things that would jeopardize his presidency and ruin his family's reputation."

Haley chewed slowly. Needing a few moments to gather her thoughts, she considered her best friend's words. Yesterday, Joshua had implied that Ashton was as shady as a mobster—but Haley wasn't buying it. Not for a second. Whatever Becca's fiancé thought he knew about Ashton couldn't be so bad. The Rollinses were a respected family who had supported local charities for decades, and Haley was glad she'd met Ashton at the Millionaire Moguls meeting. He was throwing his support behind The Aunt Penny Foundation, and that was good enough for her. The organization was strapped for cash and could use a man of Ashton's influence in their corner.

"Everyone has secrets, Becca. Even you."

"No, I don't. I'm an open book."

Haley wiped her mouth with a napkin. "Oh, really? So, Josh knows about the time you went skinny-dipping with your cousins at that deserted beach in Tijuana?"

"Hell no!" she said with a laugh. "I'm taking that secret with me to the grave!"

"My point exactly. We've all done things we regret. Me, you and even Josh."

"Girl, I agree with you, but Josh is on a mission to unearth the truth."

"If Josh has something to say why hasn't he come forward? Where's his proof?"

"So far, it's nothing but hearsay."

"Then Josh should keep his opinions to himself." Haley picked up her mug and sipped her coffee. Her gaze strayed to the window. Dark clouds sailed across the sky, obscuring the sun, and a blustery summer wind shook the plants and trees. Haley hoped it didn't rain. She had errands to do at lunchtime, and she didn't want her ivory dress and wedge sandals to get soaked.

"Do you want to date Ashton? Is that why you're defending him?" Becca asked.

To avoid answering the question, Haley took a bite of her bagel and studied the children's artwork displayed on the walls. "I know Ashton's *way* out of my league, but we really hit it off last night, and I want to see him again."

"Out of your league?" Becca puckered her lips and shook her head, her chandelier earrings swinging furiously back and forth. "Don't be ridiculous. You're the total package."

Haley nodded, but deep down, she knew she'd never measure up to Ashton's ex-girlfriends. And there were a lot. Last night in bed she'd made the mistake of Googling him and found hundreds of images of the dashing Miami bachelor with women who looked like runway models.

"Be careful, Haley. Take things slow. Don't rush into anything."

"Said the girl who got engaged only *weeks* after meeting her new boyfriend."

"Touché," Becca said with a laugh. "But when a girl knows, she knows, and the first time Josh kissed me I knew he was the only man for me. I tried to fight my feelings and keep him at bay, but he easily won me over, and I'm glad he did."

"Girl, stop! You sound like an online dating commercial!"

Stars filled Becca's eyes. "I love my man and he loves me, and that's all that matters."

They'd been friends for years, and Haley couldn't recall ever seeing Becca this happy. It warmed her heart that after countless disappointments, her BFF had met someone who cherished her.

"Are you seeing Ashton again tonight?"

Yes, and I can't wait! she thought, resisting the urge to break out in song. Feeling giddy, Haley pursed her lips together to trap a squeal inside her mouth. Now she was the one with the dreamy expression on her face and the goofy, lopsided grin. "I told Ashton I was volunteering at the soup kitchen, and he offered to help out."

"Yeah, right, and I'm going to remain celibate until my wedding night!"

"Why is it so hard for you to believe that Ashton's volunteering tonight?"

"There's no way in hell he's going down to the mission to feed the homeless." Standing, Becca dumped her trash in the garbage can. "He's a zillionaire. That's beneath him."

"It shouldn't be. If the Obamas can serve dinner to the homeless, *anyone* can."

"Good point, but men of Ashton's stature usually don't. Just sayin'."

"That shouldn't be the case," Haley argued, rising to her feet. "Everyone, regardless of their social status, has a duty to help those in need. Aunt Penny always says, 'Giving to the less fortunate nourishes the soul,' and I wholeheartedly agree."

A grin curled Becca's lips. "Does that mean you're going to *give* Ashton some tonight?"

"You're a mess, you know that?" Haley rinsed her dishes, put them in the dishwasher and slammed it shut with her hip. "What happened to the kind, sweet girl I used to know?"

"She got engaged to a man with six-pack abs!" Becca shrieked, fanning her face.

"You've changed for the worse," Haley teased. "You used to talk about social issues and saving up to buy your first home, and now all you talk about is sex."

"It's not my fault my fiancé's fine as hell. I can't help myself!"

Giggling, the women left the staff room arm in arm, swapping stories about the rivals of the Millionaire Moguls of Miami.

Three hours later, Haley was sitting at her desk, buried under a mountain of paperwork, listening to her favorite radio station. Jazz music was playing on Lite FM, and thanks to her aromatherapy candle the air smelled of roses and lavender. She'd accomplished a lot since arriving at her office that morning, but still had a hefty to-do list. Haley was craving another cup of coffee, but she decided to finish editing the monthly newsletter before taking a break.

Her gaze fell across the picture frame on her desk. The photograph was taken last summer, with all of the students in the mentorship program, and Haley marveled at how different Sienna looked. In the picture the teen was laughing, but these days she rarely smiled. Curious how she was doing, Haley made a mental note to call her at lunchtime.

The phone rang. Recognizing it was an internal call, she answered on the second ring.

"I hope you're sitting down, because I have bad news."

It was Mr. MacTavish, the foundation's part-time accountant, and Haley could tell by the strain in his voice that he was upset. "Calvin, what is it?"

"The check we received last week from Mr. and Mrs. Polanski bounced," he explained. "The bank just called to inform me, and I wanted to give you a heads-up about it."

It wasn't the first time a check had bounced, and since it probably wouldn't be the last, Haley took a deep breath and channeled positive thoughts. "How much was the check for?"

"A hundred thousand dollars."

The phone slipped from her hand, but Haley caught it before it hit the desk. A burning sensation warmed her chest, and knots formed in her stomach. She loved her job and couldn't imagine ever returning to the corporate world, but she was tired of donors letting them down. And she could do without living paycheck to paycheck as well. The nonprofit sector was not for the faint of heart, and if Haley didn't love her staff and the students they mentored she would've thrown in the towel years ago.

Telling herself there was nothing she couldn't handle, Haley said, "We received several checks last week. Did they all bounce?"

"No, thankfully, the other three cleared just fine."

Haley sighed in relief. "So, we're in good shape, then? Everything's okay?"

"Not exactly. Without those funds, we'll have to veto the Third Annual Girls' Day Extravaganza in September. We just can't afford it."

"No way. We can't do that. The students are pumped about the event. Calvin, we're not canceling."

"We have to. We have no choice."

"Becca and everyone else on the team has worked tirelessly to organize the event, and we can't disappoint the community," she said, raising her voice to prove she meant business. "Parents are counting on us, our girls too, and I won't let them down."

"Haley, your heart's in the right place, and I know how passionate you are about the foundation, but the numbers don't lie. If we don't cancel Girls' Day and tighten our spending going forward, The Aunt Penny Foundation will have to close its doors forever."

His words were a powerful blow, like a fist to the gut.

"We've been operating in the red for years, but we can't go on like this much longer."

"Calvin, don't talk like that."

"I'm not trying to dampen your spirits—"

"Then don't. Give me the numbers, so I know exactly where we stand."

Haley grabbed her ballpoint pen and made notes in her agenda, diligently writing down everything Calvin said about the finances. "I'll think of something," she promised, refusing to concede defeat. "I'll find another donor. A hundred donors if that's what it takes."

Calvin chuckled, and his hearty laugh temporarily brightened her mood.

"We've worked together for years. I should know by now not to doubt you," he said. "You always come through. That's what makes you a great CEO. You're a go-getter who's a hundred percent committed to this foundation, and the best person to lead us."

"Thanks for the vote of confidence, Calvin, and for bringing me up to speed on the finances. I'll call you once I have some fabulous new donors lined up."

"Sounds great. I look forward to hearing from you soon. Enjoy the rest of your day."

Enjoy the rest of the day? Fat chance of that happening, she thought, dropping the phone on the cradle and her face in her hands. A country music song was now playing on the radio. The female singer was lamenting the loss of her no-good, cheating boyfriend, and Haley wanted to gag. *You think* you *have problems? Try living in my world!*

What was she going to do? Haley wanted to call Aunt Penny, but thought better of it. Her aunt needed to rest. Home recovering after having a mild heart attack weeks earlier, Aunt Penny insisted she was fine, but her doctor was concerned about her declining health, as were Haley, Becca and everyone at the foundation. Aunt Penny used to be a regular fixture at the office, dropping by weekly with baked goods and treats for the staff, but these days she spent her time napping and knitting in her favorite chair.

Drumming her fingernails on the desk, racking her brain for answers, Haley considered returning to Fisher Island. Going door-to-door to solicit donations was risky, and since she didn't want to make enemies of Ashton's wealthy neighbors she abandoned the thought.

An image of the handsome COO with the dark skin, chiseled features and megawatt smile flashed in her mind. He spoke about causes and issues that were important to her, and was passionate about helping others. Ashton was a doer, someone who made things happen, and Haley could use his advice. Should she call him? Should she ask the Millionaire Moguls for help? Begging didn't sit right with her, not even on behalf of the foundation, so Haley considered other options that didn't involve her dreamy, brown-eyed crush.

Ten people with deep pockets, she decided. That's all she needed to reach her goal.

Feeling hopeful, she opened her drawer, grabbed her address book and flipped it open. Time to work her magic, because there was no way in hell she was canceling the Girls' Day Extravaganza. The students were worth it, and she wasn't going to let them down.

Names and faces flashed in her mind. Haley thought of all the charity events The Aunt Penny Foundation had hosted over the years, of all the people who'd supported the organization since its inception, and hoped they'd come through for her one more time.

Swallowing her pride, she swiped the phone off the cradle, prepared to say and do anything to keep the foundation afloat, and dialed the first number in her address book.

Chapter 5

It was true what they said, Ashton thought, opening the front door of the Miami Soup Kitchen and marching inside. A man *would* do anything to impress a woman, even volunteer on a Friday night.

Entering the center, Ashton took in his surroundings. Sparsely decorated, with potted lights and chipped tables, the dining room needed a fresh coat of paint. It was a dingy space with an unsavory scent, and if Ashton wasn't romantically interested in Haley he'd be in his car, heading back to Fisher Island to barbecue on his new grill.

Ashton shoved his keys into the pocket of his slacks. He'd driven the Porsche again tonight, in part to impress Haley and to prove to himself it wasn't haunted. Thankfully, he'd had no visions of Mia or the accident during the thirty-minute drive from his office. Thoughts of Haley, though, had consumed his mind. More excited than a kid on Christmas Day, Ashton could hardly wait to see the petite beauty. He hoped she'd change her mind and have drinks with him at the Rooftop Bar after dinner.

The sound of boisterous laughter drew Ashton's attention to the back of the room. A group of teenagers were playing cards, several people were texting and chatting on their cell phones and two heavyset men were arguing in Spanish.

"You look lost."

Ashton glanced over his shoulder, spotted a short, Caucasian man standing in the kitchen and nodded his head in greeting.

"How can I help you, son?" The man's face was lined with wrinkles, and he spoke with a lisp.

"I'm supposed to meet Haley Adams here. By any chance, have you seen her?"

"Nope." Shrugging, the man put on a hair net and an apron. "Don't think Haley's coming tonight. I overheard one of the other volunteers say she has other plans."

He felt so disappointed his shoulders sagged. He'd wasted his time coming to the shelter. He should have stayed at work, perfecting his speech for the Caracas Business Summit instead of driving across town to volunteer. Why hadn't Haley called to give him a heads-up? Ashton wondered. Had she forgotten about him already? Was she on a date with another man?

Ashton turned to leave, noticed everyone in the room was staring at him and changed his mind. Since he had no other plans, he decided to stay and help out. Taking off his sunglasses, he tucked them into his back pocket. Having a wardrobe in his office, he'd changed from his tailored suit into a striped Ralph Lauren shirt, black pants and leather sandals. Feeling overdressed in his designer threads, he made a mental note to wear jeans the next time he came to the shelter.

"I'm Ashton," he said, approaching the kitchen counter.

"Good to meet you." The man in the apron smiled, revealing chipped, coffee-stained teeth.

"Everyone calls me Monty."

"I'm here to volunteer. What do you need me to do?"

Surprise flashed in his eyes, but he gestured to the hallway. "Take out the garbage in the bathrooms, mop the floor and, if it's not too much trouble, set up some more tables."

"No trouble at all, Monty."

For an hour, Ashton helped clean and organize the dining room. Giving back to the community made him feel proud, as if he was making a difference, and cracking jokes with the other volunteers put him in a good mood. Ashton was standing beside the window, scrubbing maple syrup off the walls when he heard a familiar voice. Haley's. Curious, he dropped his rag into the bucket of soapy water and peered into the kitchen. There she was. Standing at the stove, stirring a metal pot with a wooden spoon, flirting with a male volunteer.

His eyes narrowed and the muscles in his jaw quivered. Ashton wanted to march into the kitchen and pull Haley away from the stranger, but he knew it was a bad idea. He didn't want her to think he was a hothead, and if he made a scene she'd lose respect for him.

Friendly and effervescent, Haley was the kind of person who made friends wherever she went, and it was obvious the stranger had a crush on her. The man was following her around the kitchen like a lost puppy. Ashton didn't blame him. Dressed in a pink cardigan and a belted sundress, Haley looked pretty and youthful, and the more Ashton watched her the more he longed to kiss her. *I'll hang tight*, he decided. *And let her come to me.*

Ten minutes later, his patience paid off. Ashton was in the storage room, grabbing a case of bottled water, when Haley rushed in and stopped abruptly.

"Ashton, you're here!"

Her wide-eyed expression made him chuckle.

"I got here hours ago." Deciding to take a break, he put the case of water on the floor. "You didn't see me hard at work in the dining room with the other volunteers?"

"No. I got here late and headed straight for the kitchen."

I know, he thought sourly. *I saw you and your buddy yukking it up.*

"How's the gumbo coming along?"

"Good. It's almost done." Stepping past him, Haley searched the shelves and grabbed a bottle of seasoning salt and cayenne pepper. "Ten more minutes and it's gumbo time!"

"I'm anxious to try it. I hope it's as good as you say it is."

"You're going to love it," she promised. "You just wait and see."

"I'll save you a seat at my table." Ashton tried to sound casual, as if the seating arrangements were no big deal, but he'd come to the center to spend time with Haley, not watch her flirt with other men. "We can eat together."

"I'd like that. You can tell me about your day, and I can fill you in on all the exciting new programs we're launching at The Aunt Penny Foundation in the fall."

"Or we could talk about us."

All at once, without considering the consequences of his actions, Ashton slammed the door shut with one hand and pulled her to his chest with the other. Consumed with desire, he backed her into the wall, stroking and caressing her hips. The spices fell from her hands and rolled across the floor. Before Ashton knew what he was doing he was kissing her, passionately, desperately, groaning into her warm, sweet mouth. He pressed his lips to hers, savoring the taste of her moist lips, turned on by how juicy they were.

Haley, however, didn't return his kiss. Her body tensed

against his, and she pulled out of his arms. Panting, she braced her hands against his chest. "Ashton, what are you doing?"

"Kissing you. Isn't it obvious?"

Her eyes narrowed and her hands fell to her sides.

"You didn't like it?" he asked, curious why she was giving him the cold shoulder.

"That's not the point. I'm not that girl—"

"What girl?"

"A girl who has casual hookups. I don't do one-night stands, or jump from guy to guy."

"Good, because I want us to be exclusive."

"After one date? But we hardly know each other."

"That's the point. That's why I'm here. To spend time with you."

Haley studied him intently. "Do you always say exactly what's on your mind?"

"Always. I'm a Rollins. It's in my DNA!" Ashton said with a hearty laugh. "I don't believe in beating around the bush. I tell it like it is, no matter what."

"Relationships don't happen overnight, Ashton. They take time and commitment."

Every part of his body ached for her, but he kept his hands to himself.

"I don't want to rush into anything…"

Her voice was so quiet Ashton strained to hear what she was saying. "Haley, what's going on? Why are you keeping me at arm's length?"

"I've been celibate for over a year," she blurted out, toying with the buttons on her cardigan. "I don't want to repeat the mistakes I made in past relationships, so if you can't respect the personal choice I've made we should just be friends."

"I respect your decision." Taking her hand in his, he gave

it a soft squeeze. "And I'm cool with it. Sleeping with you is the furthest thing from my mind."

Liar! shouted his conscience. *Sex is the* only *thing on your mind!*

Moving closer, Ashton drew her back into his arms. He loved feeling her body against his. Stroking her skin, he stepped back and marveled at her natural beauty. Her almond-shaped eyes, her high cheekbones, her plump lips. Her makeup was simple and her floral fragrance, a soothing, calming scent.

"Ashton, you're staring."

"I can't help it. You're a captivating woman whose inner beauty shines bright and I want to know everything there is to know about you."

"I feel the same way. You're unlike anyone I've ever met, and I'm intrigued by you."

To make her laugh, Ashton said, "Of course you are. Rollins men are in a league of their own, and don't you forget it."

"And humble, too? Wow, I hit the jackpot," she quipped, her tone thick with sarcasm.

They shared a laugh, and Ashton knew Haley was enjoying their flirtatious banter.

"What have you done to me?" he asked her. "One date, and you've turned my world upside down."

"I have? But I haven't done anything."

"You're wrong. You have," he insisted. "I left the office early, and I'm volunteering at a soup kitchen for the first time in my life. If that isn't a miracle, I don't know what is."

Their eyes locked, and Ashton moved closer, swallowed the space between them.

"I better get back to the kitchen before Monty skins my hide for burning the gumbo."

"Not so fast," he said, sliding in front of the door. "We have to redo our first kiss."

"Why? What was wrong with the first one?"

"Everything. You were tense and preoccupied and it ended abruptly."

Haley raised an index finger in the air. "One kiss."

"I thought you'd never ask."

Caressing her cheeks, he drew his finger against her soft, smooth skin.

Parting her lips, Haley touched her mouth to his, tentatively, as if she was testing the waters. Ashton dove right in. He feasted on her lips, relishing the taste of her mouth for the second time in minutes. Ashton wanted to spend the rest of the night making out with Haley, but he remembered she wanted to take things slow, and reluctantly ended the kiss. Dinner had started, and he didn't want them to get caught necking in the pantry.

"That was nice," Haley said.

"I aim to please." Ashton winked. "We can practice more after dinner."

Bending down, she scooped up the items she'd dropped on the floor. "We'll talk later."

"You can count on it."

Ashton opened the door and stepped aside. Licking his lips, he watched Haley sashay down the corridor, mesmerized by her sexy, hypnotic strut. Yes, he loved giving back to the community, he thought with a lopsided grin. It was very rewarding indeed!

"I'd sooner be a prisoner of war than remarry," Monty joked, a toothpick dangling from between his thin, chapped lips. "I was shackled to a Ukrainian she-devil for nine long years and there's no way in hell I'm going down that road again."

Shrieks and chuckles rippled around the table. Ashton noticed everyone was laughing, except Haley, and wondered what was on her mind. He was sitting across from her, eating his second bowl of gumbo, savoring every bite. The thick stew, rich with spices, vegetables and shrimp, was delicious, and Ashton planned to help himself to another bowl.

"Marriage can be a wonderful thing," Haley argued, addressing the elderly cook. "My parents got divorced when I was a teenager, but my grandparents have been happily married for over fifty years and my grandpa Earl still dotes on my grandmother—"

"He drinks hard liquor, doesn't he?" Monty said.

Snickers filled the air, and Ashton decided the wisecracking cook needed his own HBO comedy special. During dinner, he'd entertained the group with stories about growing up in Alabama and the years he'd spent in the military. Their conversation was loud and spirited, and the pop music playing on the stereo system enhanced the festive mood inside the center.

"I don't know why everyone is so anti-marriage these days," Haley said. "Building a life with someone is a worthwhile endeavor and one day I hope to be a wife and mother."

Ashton heard his cell phone ring, glanced down at the table and noted the number on the screen. Scowling, he pressed the decline button and finished eating his gumbo. He didn't want to talk to his dad. Not now. For the past two days, Alexander had been badgering him to confront Joshua, but he'd refused. It was his life, his decision, and he was sick and tired of arguing with his dad about Prescott George. He was having a great time with Haley and the other volunteers, and he wasn't going to let his dad ruin his good mood.

Still, his thoughts returned to weeks earlier. In June, at a private event at a posh steakhouse, he'd butted heads with Joshua about the public relations department of Prescott George. Joshua wanted to advertise publicly, to post and tweet about various events, but Ashton wanted to maintain the exclusivity of the seventy-five-year-old organization. In his opinion, media blasts were tacky, a desperate attempt for attention, and they had no place in Prescott George. A heated argument had ensued, and if Daniel Cobb hadn't intervened they probably would have come to blows. Weeks later, Ashton was still pissed about the accusations Joshua had made.

"There's no such thing as too much publicity," Joshua had said, folding his arms.

"We're Prescott George. We don't need *any* publicity," Ashton had shot back.

"You're a dictator who's stuck in the dark ages."

"And you're an obstinate jerk with a chip on his shoulder."

"You need to listen to the members, instead of ignoring them."

Breaking free of his thoughts, Ashton spooned shrimp into his mouth and chewed slowly. Reflecting on his five-year presidency, he wondered if Joshua's criticism was well-founded. Had he lost touch with the members? Was he a stubborn, ineffective leader? Lost in his own world, he didn't realize Haley was talking to him until she touched his arm.

"You agree with me, right, Ashton?"

Feeling guilty for zoning out, he nodded his head. "Absolutely."

"Marriage is a partnership, not a prison sentence," Haley continued.

"The older I get, the more I want what my parents have," Ashton confessed, speaking from the heart. "Life is about more than just working and making money, and I'd love to have someone to grow old with."

The women at the table beamed, but the men groaned.

"Don't do it, young buck," advised Monty, adamantly shaking his head. "Marriage is a death sentence, and if things go sour with your wife, which they inevitably will, you could lose half your fortune and that's a steep price to pay."

All across the table utensils dropped, eyes popped and jaws fell open.

"My fortune?" Ashton repeated, appearing nonchalant though he was shocked by the cook's comment. "What makes you think I have money?"

Everyone straightened in their seats and glanced from Ashton to Monty.

"Just because I'm old and gray doesn't mean I don't know who the movers and shakers in Miami are."

A female volunteer with gray hair and glasses leaned forward in her seat. "Don't keep us in suspense, Ashton. How much is your family worth? A million? Five million?" When he didn't respond, the woman gulped. "Ten million?"

"Leave him alone," said a man who'd told the group he was a city bus driver. "You're embarrassing him."

"Shame on you for trying to put the moves on Ashton." Monty wagged a finger in the woman's round, plump face. "It doesn't matter how much he's worth. You're old enough to be his mother, and contrary to what you think black *does* crack."

Everyone laughed long and hard. Monty announced it was time to clean up, and the group picked up their empty cups and plates, and left the table.

"Sorry about that," Haley said, wearing an apologetic smile. "Bertha was just joking."

"No worries. It isn't the first time someone asked me

about my net worth, and it probably won't be the last. On the upside, at least she didn't whip out her cell phone and Google my name. I hate when that happens."

Haley had a guilty expression on her face but her voice was full of surprise. "That's crazy. Women actually do that?"

"You don't know the half of it, but I'll tell you all about my disastrous dating history later when we go for drinks at the Rooftop Bar."

"No can do. I'm sorry. After I clean up, I'm staying to help Monty and the other volunteers plan the annual Labor Day brunch," she explained, stacking their empty plates at the end of the table.

"I don't mind sticking around a little longer."

Haley shook her head. "Please don't. Our meetings usually last a couple hours."

Ashton finished his food and wiped his mouth with a napkin. In his peripheral vision, he saw Haley's male friend watching them from across the room, and draped an arm around her chair. The stranger was a thorn in his side. Every time Ashton looked up, the man was making eyes at Haley. Buzz off, he thought, glaring at the competition. Couldn't he see that she was taken?

Ashton openly admired Haley. She was in a class all by herself, and not just because of her striking good looks. Haley was likeable, gregarious and a great conversationalist who loved to argue and debate about current events. Her intelligence appealed to him and was, in fact, a huge turn-on.

"Come on. I'll walk you to your car."

Ashton chuckled. It was the last thing he'd expected her to say, but he took her outstretched hand and allowed her to lead him through the front doors. The air smelled of rain, but the sky was free of clouds and full of twinkling stars.

"This is a first," he said, slipping an arm around her waist. "I don't think I've ever had anyone escort me to my car."

Winking, Haley patted his cheek. "That's just the kind of girl I am."

"This was great," he said. "Thanks for inviting me. It was fun."

"Does that mean you'll volunteer again?"

"For sure, but next time I'm helping you in the kitchen. I need that gumbo recipe!"

Hearing her giggle made Ashton grin.

"Text me when you get home so I know you arrived safely."

"Okay, Mom," he said, chuckling. "I'll pick you up tomorrow at one o'clock and we'll eat before the game."

"It's a date. Bye, Ashton."

Haley gave him a peck on the lips, then walked across the parking lot before Ashton could wrap her up in his arms and deepen the kiss. He wanted to call out to her, but since he didn't want to look desperate he unlocked the Porsche and slid inside.

The night had been a success, and Ashton suddenly felt hopeful and excited. Haley was the reason. They had a strong connection and incredible chemistry, and it would be just a matter of time before they were lovers. He wouldn't push her, though. It had to happen on her terms. Mentally planning their second date, he sped through the parking lot, anxious to get home to make the necessary arrangements.

Chapter 6

"Haley, when are you going to let me take you out on a date?" Flashing a toothy grin, the slim, blond doorman at Regency Condominiums opened the front door of the eighteen-floor building located in a quiet, suburban neighborhood of Miami. "You know you're the only girl for me."

"Speaking of girls, how are your wife and your three daughters?"

Dodging her gaze, he coughed into his fist.

Haley didn't need his help, but she allowed him to take her grocery bags and followed him through the glass-and-marble lobby. Built with luxury and convenience in mind, the apartment had twenty-four-hour security and an on-site spa, fitness center and café. The staff was courteous and attentive, and Aunt Penny raved to all her friends about the upscale condominium. In spite of her recent health scare, she refused to move to a nursing home, insisting she could take care of herself, but Haley was worried about her declining health.

Noting the time on the wall clock, she hoped Aunt Penny was up for a visit. She hadn't seen her in several days and wanted to check up on her before her date. At the thought of the dreamy COO happiness flooded her heart. That kiss. It was all she could think about. The memory of it burned bright in her mind. On the surface she'd remained calm, but the moment he'd touched her desire had exploded inside her body. Even now, she yearned for him. Her feelings for Ashton—her overwhelming attraction to him—shocked her, but Haley was determined to keep her wits about her at the Firebirds game that afternoon. Her instincts told her Ashton was a stand-up guy, and until he showed her otherwise she was going to enjoy his company—and his kisses.

"Every time I see you, you look more beautiful," the doorman said.

Returning to the present, Haley strangled a groan. As if she'd ever date a married man, she thought, dropping her keys inside her tote bag. The doorman had asked her out weeks earlier, but thanks to Aunt Penny she'd learned about his no-good cheating ways and canceled their lunch date at a Greek restaurant. Since Haley didn't want to be a sister-wife or a home-wrecker, she took her bags from the doorman without replying and boarded the elevator.

Hearing her cell phone ring, Haley fished it out of her purse. Becca! Dying to speak to her best friend, she swiped her finger across the screen and put her cell to her ear. "Guess who showed up at the soup kitchen last night?" she asked, feeling a rush of pride.

Becca shrieked. "Ashton went? No way! I don't believe you!"

"It's true. He set up tables, served supper and even mopped the floors."

"Wow, I'm impressed. Ashton must really like you..."

The elevator pinged and the doors slid open on the ninth floor.

Haley wanted to tell Becca everything—about their first kiss, their marathon phone conversation after she'd arrived home last night and their afternoon date—but it wasn't the right time or place to have a heart-to-heart conversation with her BFF about Ashton.

"I want to hear everything," Becca continued, her tone filled with giddy excitement. "Are you going to see him again? Are you falling for him? Do you think Ashton could be 'The One'?"

Grabbing her things, she exited the elevator. "Becca, I'll call you back. I just got to Aunt Penny's, and if she sees me on my cell she'll lecture me about how they cause health problems."

"Wait! Don't go! I'm with Josh and he wants to speak to you."

Haley stared down at the phone. "About what?"

Becca giggled. "Ashton, of course. Hold on. I'll pass him the phone."

"Becca, no! I don't think that's a good idea—" Before Haley could finish her thought, a male voice filled the line, and she broke off speaking.

"Morning, Haley. How's life treating you?"

"Good. How are you?"

"I'm engaged to the most amazing woman in the world. How do you *think* I'm doing?"

Haley smiled. Couldn't help it. Joshua had a way with words, was more charming than a Hollywood actor, and Haley suspected Becca was cuddled up beside him, beaming like a pageant winner on center stage. "Becca said you wanted to speak to me about Ashton. What's up?"

Cradling her cell between her ear and her shoulder, Haley leaned against the wall and listened intently. Sunlight streamed through the floor-to-ceiling windows; glass vases filled with colored tulips sweetened the air with their strong, fragrant scent.

"Haley, I need a favor."

Holding her breath, she felt her mouth go dry and every muscle inside her body tense up.

"Next time you speak to Ashton ask him to phone me."

"Why? Surely you have his cell number."

"I've called and texted him numerous times, but he hasn't responded."

She wasn't surprised. Joshua was trying to unseat him as president of the Millionaire Moguls. No wonder Ashton wouldn't talk to him!

Choosing her words carefully, she said, "Josh, I can't. I don't want to get in the middle of your feud with Ashton. Doing so could jeopardize Prescott George's support, and The Aunt Penny Foundation is in desperate need of their financial help."

"I assure you it won't." He spoke in a confident voice. "Just ask Ashton to call me."

"I don't know, Josh. I have a bad feeling about this."

"Please, Haley. I need your help."

"Why don't you ask one of the other members to speak to Ashton on your behalf? Why me?"

"Because he likes you, and a man will do anything for the woman he's dating."

A smile tickled her lips. The word *no* echoed in her mind, but the word *yes* fell from her mouth. "Okay," she conceded reluctantly. "I'll give him the message."

"Thanks, Haley. You're a lifesaver."

Her doubts remained, but she pushed them aside. "No problem."

"Enjoy the rest of your day."

She certainly would. She was seeing Ashton in a few

hours and she couldn't wait. Ending the call, Haley dropped her cell into her purse. *What did I just agree to?* she thought, taking a deep breath.

Pressed for time, she shook off her doubts and rushed down the hall. She had to hurry. She still had to go home and get ready for her date. Stopping in front of apartment 906, Haley jabbed the buzzer and waited for her aunt to answer.

Aunt Penny's neighbors, an elderly Indian couple wearing traditional Hindu clothes, nodded in greeting as they exited their suite. Intrigued, Haley watched them with growing interest. They'd been married for decades and had dozens of grandchildren, but they gazed longingly at each other as they boarded the elevator. *That's what I want. Someone who loves and adores me, and puts me first.*

Surfacing from her thoughts, Haley jabbed the doorbell for the second time. Seconds passed. Moving closer to the door, she put her ear to it and listened intently. Nothing. There was no way her aunt was still asleep. A morning person who loved watching the sunrise from her balcony, Aunt Penny never went to bed late and rarely slept in. Was she okay? Was she having chest pains again? Did she need medical help?

Concerned, Haley opened her purse, took out the spare key Aunt Penny had given her months earlier and unlocked the door. Clean and spacious, the three-bedroom apartment had pale pink walls, vintage furniture and antiques, and decorative floor lamps. It had a calming vibe and more African-American art than a museum.

Haley put the groceries on the kitchen counter and set out in search of her aunt. The apartment smelled of air freshener, an episode of *Celebrity Family Feud* was playing on the old, bubble-style TV and library books were piled high on the coffee table.

"Hello?" she called. "Aunt Penny? Are you here?"

The bathroom door swung open, and Penelope "Penny" Washington shuffled out, humming a gospel hymn. With her wiry gray hair, dark brown eyes that missed nothing and full figure, she resembled the late, great Maya Angelou. "Honey, of course I'm home. I'm eighty-eight years old. Where else would I be?"

Sighing in relief, Haley threw her arms around the woman and kissed her cheek. "I got worried when you didn't answer the door," she confessed. "I thought maybe you were sick."

"You worry too much."

"I have reason to. You were rushed to the hospital a couple months ago, remember?"

"That was then, and this is now. I'm as fit as a fiddle." To prove it, Aunt Penny danced in place, swaying her body from side to side. "See, baby girl, I'm the hottest thing around!"

Giggling, Haley admired her aunt's outfit. Like many Florida "nanas," Aunt Penny favored tracksuits and sneakers, and never left home without her leather fanny pack. Intelligent and insightful, with a keen mind, she'd invested wisely in telecommunications stocks decades earlier and reaped massive dividends when she'd retired as a management analyst. Looking at her, it was hard to believe the senior was a multimillionaire, but she was. If she'd called Aunt Penny yesterday about the bounced check, she would have covered the cost, but since Haley didn't want anyone to think she was taking advantage of her she'd worked the phones all afternoon, calling in favors, speaking to donors and local celebrities. Her persistence had paid off. Tomorrow, she was having brunch with a successful businessman, and if everything went according to plan she'd leave the restaurant with a six-figure donation for The Aunt Penny Foundation.

"Dear, it's good to see you. What brings you by?"

Haley gestured to the table. "I brought you groceries and some more knitting magazines. Sienna and I went to a garage sale last week, and we bought up everything they had."

"And people say this generation is hopeless," she said, affectionately patting her cheek. "You're not. You're the most thoughtful young person I know."

Yawning, Haley rubbed her eyes. "It was nothing."

"Honey, you look tired." Cupping her chin, Aunt Penny spoke in a sympathetic voice. "You haven't been getting enough sleep. How come?"

Because Ashton and I talked for hours last night. Worried her aunt would see the truth on her face, she opened the grocery bags and put everything away in the fridge. "I was up late."

"Doing what, pray tell? Working?"

"No, talking to a friend," she explained, remembering how much fun she'd had on the phone, joking and laughing with Ashton. "By the time I fell asleep it was time to wake up."

Aunt Penny raised an eyebrow. "A friend, huh? Tell me more about him."

"What makes you think it's a guy?"

"Lucky guess."

Inching away from the table, Haley glanced at her wrist and tapped the front of her gold watch. "Wow, look at the time. I have to run, but I'll call you—"

"Surely you're not too busy to have a cup of tea with your favorite aunt?"

Aunt Penny turned on the kettle, then pointed at a wrought-iron chair. "Honey, sit. I want to hear all about you and Ashton Rollins."

A gasp shot out of Haley's mouth. "Who told you I'm dating Ashton Rollins?"

"A little birdie told me."

Becca! Annoyed, she pursed her lips together to trap a curse inside. *I wonder how much jail time I'd get for strangling my ex–best friend*, she thought, reluctantly sitting down at the table. While Aunt Penny shuffled around the kitchen, making breakfast, Haley chatted about the center, but her aunt swiftly navigated the conversation back to her dating life—specifically, her relationship with Ashton.

"Honey, don't rush into anything," she advised in a stern voice. "Take the time to get to know him as a person, and above all else, listen to your heart."

Haley took a bite of her cranberry muffin and chewed slowly. Sitting with Aunt Penny, talking and eating, reminded Haley of all the times she'd spent at the woman's house as a tween. If not for Aunt Penny's love, guidance and support she probably would have ended up in the wrong crowd or, worse, been a high school dropout.

"If you hook up with Ashton he won't respect you."

"Hook up?" she repeated, amused by her aunt's jargon. "What do *you* know about hooking up?"

Aunt Penny raised an eyebrow. "Don't let the wrinkles fool you. I'm *very* hip."

The women laughed.

"Patience is the key to lasting happiness," Aunt Penny continued. "And don't feel bad about making him wait to have an intimate relationship, either. It's your body, your decision, and if Ashton cares about you he won't mind waiting. A gentleman never does."

"Did that approach work for you in your past relationships?"

"No, unfortunately, I was a fast, young thing when I was

your age, hopping from one guy to the next, and it took me a long time to get my act together, but thankfully I did."

"*You* were a fast, young thing?" she joked, shaking her head. "Say it ain't so!"

Sadness suddenly filled Aunt Penny's eyes. "Loneliness drove me into the arms of a wealthy married man, and although our arrangement worked wonderfully for him, it almost ruined my life."

Shocked and curious, Haley hung on to every word that came out of her aunt's mouth.

"I lost friends and family members because of our affair. I thought having a man was all that mattered, but it's better to be single and content than have a man and be miserable."

"You dated a married man?" she asked, stunned by her aunt's words.

Staring down at her slender, wrinkled hands, Aunt Penny slowly nodded her head. "Yes, and even after all these years I'm still deeply ashamed about it. I caused his family great pain, and if I could go back in time I never would have gotten involved with him," she confessed. "That's why I warned you about that young, charming doorman. You're a smart cookie, but I didn't want you to make the same mistakes I made."

Moved by her aunt's story, Haley reached out and squeezed her hand.

"Listen to your wise, old aunt," Aunt Penny said with a weak smile. "I know Ashton's a catch and every woman in this city is pining for him, but don't rush into anything. Trust your instincts."

"I will," she promised. "Thanks for the talk, Aunt Penny. It was just what I needed to hear."

"Anytime, but next time you come over bring some wine. It goes great with tea."

Laughing, Haley tucked her feet under her bottom and

slid her hands around her oversized mug. She glanced down at her cell phone, saw that she had a new text message and punched in her password. Goose bumps flooded her skin as she read Ashton's heartfelt words.

I just want you to know I'm thinking about you.

His message gave her a rush. Made her want to jump up and dance around Aunt Penny's apartment. Her aunt was watching her, and since Haley didn't want her to know how much she liked Ashton she tempered her excitement. They'd only known each other for a few weeks, and if she gushed about how sweet and romantic he was Aunt Penny would be all up in her business.

In a playful mood, she texted back: Thinking about me, or my gumbo?

Sipping her tea Haley listened as Aunt Penny told her, in precise detail, about the afghan blankets her knitting club were making to donate to the women's shelter. Her cell phone lit up, drawing her attention to the table, and Ashton's response made a giggle tickle her throat.

I wish both of you were here with me right now!

Head bent, Haley was so busy typing she didn't notice Aunt Penny was standing beside her until her aunt touched her shoulder. "Honey, run along. It's obvious you're eager to see Ashton, and who am I to stand in your way?" she said, giving her a one-arm hug. "I want to meet him, so bring him over one day next week for tea."

"I can't. It's too soon. We haven't been dating long."

"If he cares about you, he'll want to meet your family."

Aunt Penny picked up the empty plates and cups, and put them in the sink.

"For now, can we keep my relationship with Ashton between me and you?" Haley asked. "I'm not ready to tell my parents yet, so please don't say anything when you talk to my mom."

"Of course." Aunt Penny nodded. "I won't say a word."

Haley knew that before she reached the elevator Aunt Penny would be on the phone, gossiping with her friends in the Senior Knitting Club, but as she exited the apartment she hoped her aunt would keep her word and not tell Melinda. Sour on love after her sixteen-year-marriage had ended in divorce, Melinda Adams thought all men were jerks, and encouraged Haley to focus on her career instead of finding Mr. Right. Talking to her mom about the opposite sex was more stressful than doing the *New York Times* Sunday crossword puzzle, and Haley shuddered to think what would happen if Aunt Penny told Melinda about Ashton.

Reaching the main floor, Haley spotted the doorman flirting with a voluptuous redhead, and thanked her lucky stars Aunt Penny had given her the scoop about him before it was too late. Feeling it was her duty to warn others about the gregarious Brazilian, she waved and said, "Bye, Matheus! Have a great weekend with your wife and kids!"

His face fell, the redhead gasped, and if looks could kill the doorman would be pushing up daisies. Haley swallowed a laugh as she sailed through the front door. Walking up the block with a pep in her step, she couldn't wait to see Ashton. He was charming. Athletic. Great with his hands. An exceptional kisser. And he wanted to be with her—a girl from the wrong side of the tracks who didn't belong in his world.

Doubts filled her, intensifying as his words played in her mind. *I want us to be exclusive... I've never been a player. I've always been a one-woman man... I know what I want, Haley, and it's you.*

Her inner voice cut through her thoughts. Did Ashton have another woman on the side like all the other men she'd met in recent months? Was he playing her? Did he mean what he'd said last night on the phone, or was it all part of his act?

Sunshine rained down from the sky, and the warm summer breeze floated through her hair. The beautiful day chased away her anxiety and she hurried toward her car as fast as her high-heel sandals could take her. For the first time in months, she was excited about her dating life, and wanted to explore her feelings for Ashton.

Deciding to trust her gut, she made up her mind not to let anyone sour her opinion of Ashton. He was a gentleman who appealed to her in every way, and Haley wasn't going to let anything stand in the way of their happiness—not even the people she loved most.

Chapter 7

Skyline Park, the newly built stadium in West Miami, was a sports enthusiast's dream. Sleek and shiny, with shops, trendy restaurants and a swank VIP lounge filled with Firebirds memorabilia, it had everything a baseball fan could want. The team had a pitiful record and seemed to be on a losing streak, but Haley was a fan so watching the game with Ashton in his luxury box on Saturday afternoon was the highlight of her week.

Haley raised her glass to her lips and tasted her pineapple rum cocktail. Seated in a cushy parlor chair, sipping the fruity drink prepared by their personal suite concierge, she tore her gaze away from the field and snuck a glance at Ashton. The Firebirds were losing miserably, down six in the bottom of the ninth, but Haley was having the time of her life. There was rose champagne, gourmet chocolate and more food than an all-you-can-eat buffet. Prior to the first pitch, Ashton had taken her to the clubhouse for a tour and it was an experience she'd never forget. On a first-name basis with everyone from the owner to the players and coaching staff, he was obviously well-liked and respected by everyone in the Firebirds organization.

"Come on!" Haley shouted, cupping her hands around her mouth. "Quit dropping the ball! This is the majors, not Little League! Firebirds, get it together or you're toast!"

"Simmer down, or security will come running," Ashton joked, resting his tumbler on the granite counter in front of him. "I know a lot of passionate fans, but you put them all to shame. How do you know so much about baseball?"

"My dad." A smile warmed her heart and curled her lips. Her parents had split up when Haley was a teenager, and although Russell Adams had remarried and had three other children, she would always be his little girl. He'd call her after almost every Firebirds game, and they'd talk for hours about their beloved team. Her parents both lived hundreds of miles away so she only saw them a couple times a year. It saddened Haley that she couldn't see them more often, but The Aunt Penny Foundation kept her very busy. "My dad lives and breathes sports, and taught me about baseball when I was still in diapers."

"It sounds like you and your dad have a special bond."

Haley nodded. "Doctors told my parents they were having a boy, so my father was shocked when I was born. He agreed to name me Haley instead of Hank, but he refused to redecorate the baseball-themed nursery or dress me in pink," she said with a laugh. "I've been a Firebirds fan since I could walk, and one of my fondest memories of my dad is when he dressed me up as Sammy Sosa for Halloween and took me trick-or-treating!"

Ashton finished his drink and signaled to the concierge.

"Oh, brother." Groaning, Haley furiously shook her head. "Espinoza overthrew the ball *again*! That's the third time this inning. This is the worst I've ever seen him play."

The concierge arrived, picked up their empty plates and left.

"Are you enjoying yourself?"

"Of course," she said. "This is fun!"

Leaning in close, he draped an arm around her shoulders. His citrus aftershave tickled her nose, and desire warmed her body. It took several deep breaths and every ounce of her self-control not to climb onto his lap and crush his lips with hers. Haley loved the idea of being in a committed relationship, but experience had taught her men only cared about one thing—bedding as many women as possible—so she had to keep her guard up or else he'd break her heart. Right before he moved on to the next girl.

"Really?" he asked. "Or are you just trying to make me feel better because the Firebirds are getting their asses kicked?"

Mischief twinkled in his eyes, and his gaze smoldered with heat and sensuality.

Haley swallowed hard. What was the question again? she thought, struggling to focus. Feeling her mouth dry, she picked up her glass and finished her cocktail. "The Firebirds have zero chance of winning this game, but there's nowhere else I'd rather be than here with you. You're great company, Mr. Rollins."

"Likewise, Ms. Adams. If you weren't here I'd be drowning my sorrows in merlot!"

They'd arrived at Skyline Park right after Ashton treated her to a delicious lunch, and once the clubhouse tour was over, they'd made themselves comfortable in the spacious, attractive suite overlooking the baseball diamond. The dark, masculine décor made Haley think of a New York cigar lounge. She'd expected the room to be packed with Ashton's friends, but to her surprise she was the only guest. It suited her fine. She didn't have to compete with anyone else for his attention, and by the time the game started they were cracking jokes like old friends.

"I hear you," Haley agreed. "Things are crazy at the foundation right now, and watching baseball with you is the perfect stress reliever."

"What's stressing you out?"

"Be careful what you ask for, because once I start talking there's just no stopping me."

"Good, because I'm all ears," he said, leaning forward in his seat. "Talk to me."

Needing to vent, Haley opened up to Ashton about the challenges she faced as CEO of The Aunt Penny Foundation. A great listener with incredible insight, he made it easy for her to confide in him about her problems. "Some of our donors don't respect me because they feel I'm too young to oversee the foundation, but I earned the right to be the boss, and not just because I'm a founding member. I've worked tirelessly for the foundation since it opened three years ago, and I'll do everything in my power to make it successful."

"That goes without saying. You're a natural-born leader, and wise beyond your years."

"That's what I keep telling them, but they don't believe me!"

Haley laughed, and Ashton did, too. Their eyes zeroed in on each other. Ashton was *It*. Dashing, suave, intelligent and sincere. Everything a woman could ever want in a man. Haley didn't care that he came from money. That didn't impress her. What mattered most to her was his character, and his words touched her deeply.

"When my dad appointed me COO eight years ago there was plenty of mumbling and grumbling at Rollins Aeronautics about me landing a senior management position, but I didn't let it faze me. Instead, I let my work ethic speak for me, and it has."

"How do you deal with employees who question your authority because you're the boss's kid?"

"I threaten to fire them, then withhold their Christmas bonuses!"

Ashton winked, and Haley knew he was kidding.

"I'm a very straightforward person, so if someone has an issue with me I call them on it. I'm second in command, and at the end of the day I have to do what's best for the company. Period. If someone doesn't like it, tough."

"I need to take a page out of your book," Haley said, impressed by his approach. "You're confident and assertive, and I bet your employees respect you as a leader."

"Most of them do, but it wasn't always that way. My first year as COO I quit at least once a day, but my dad wouldn't accept my resignation letter."

Haley whistled. "But look at you now. *Miami Business* magazine says you're a formidable leader, with a keen business mind and more swag than 007!"

"I'm impressed," he said, stroking his jaw. "You've been reading up on me."

"Of course. A good CEO always does her research."

Screams, whistles and the sound of deafening applause drew Haley's gaze to the baseball field. The kiss cam on the JumboTron panned the sold-out crowd, and fans cheered as couples hugged and kissed.

"That looks like fun." Ashton draped an arm around her shoulder. "I hope we're next."

In a blue short-sleeve shirt, slim-fit slacks and leather sandals Ashton was the sexiest man alive, and Haley relished being close to him. Like his boyish smile, his scent was intoxicating, but she couldn't resist teasing him, "Why do you need to be prompted to kiss me?"

"I don't."

"Then what are you waiting for?"

Chuckling, he reached out and swept his fingertips over the curve of her cheeks. "They say the best gifts come in small packages, and I couldn't agree more."

His lips touched hers, moving slowly and tenderly against her mouth, warming her body all over. Haley sensed Ashton was holding back, and stroked his chest through his V-neck shirt to prove she wanted him. The game forgotten, Haley lost herself in his kiss.

Closing her eyes, she devoured his mouth, enjoying the spicy flavors on his tongue. His lips were scrumptious, and his kiss sent her body into an erotic tailspin. Ashton dug his hands into her hair, playing with it, arousing and exciting her in ways she'd never imagined.

His tongue slid inside her mouth, swirling, probing and teasing, and electricity singed her skin. Every rational thought fled her mind, and Haley wanted Ashton so bad her sex tingled. Suddenly making love to Ashton was all she could think about.

Haley, get a grip! said her conscience, sounding as stern as Aunt Penny. *You're a twenty-eight-year-old woman, not a pimple-faced tween who's never been kissed!*

Shocked by her body's response to his kiss, Haley tried to regain control. It was a losing battle. His hands caressed her hips, then slid down her thighs, and she willed them to dive between her legs. Ashton kissed her until she was breathless and purring. She moaned, desperately clutched his shirt. Her feelings for him were strong, and it took everything in her not to blurt out the truth—that she wanted to make love to him right then and there in his luxury box.

Haley froze. Hearing a noise—the shrill, jarring whirl of a blender—she came to her senses and broke off the kiss. Licking her lips, she raked a hand through her hair, then straightened her purple fit-and-flare mini dress. To prove she had a fun side, she'd ditched her cardigan and accessorized her outfit with chandelier earrings, a crystal choker and peep-toe pumps. All afternoon Ashton had been complimenting her, and she'd never felt more desirable.

"I have to see you again. The sooner the better," he whispered against her ear. "I have a polo match at the Miami Polo Club tomorrow and I want you to be my date."

"Trust me, you don't." Haley wore an apologetic smile. "I don't know anything about polo, and I don't want to embarrass myself in front of your friends."

"You won't. You're graceful and sophisticated, and everyone's going to love you."

"And if they don't?"

Ashton shrugged. "Then I'll find new friends, because you're definitely a keeper."

Haley stopped breathing. His words stunned her, left her head spinning and her heart racing loud and fast. Was he serious, or just teasing her? Deciding it was the latter, she asked, "How long have you been playing polo?"

"Longer than you've been a Firebirds fan," he answered with a laugh. "My dad and grandfather both played the sport, and once I learned the rules of the game I was hooked. I took lessons as a child, and it wasn't long before I was winning tournaments."

His excitement was so infectious that as he regaled her with stories, even she had to admit the game sounded like fun. After her business meeting wrapped up, she had no other plans for Sunday, so why not spend the rest of the day hanging out with Ashton? It sure as hell beat watching old movies alone in her condo.

"I'll pick you up tomorrow at noon."

Disappointment flooded her body. "Ashton, I'm sorry, but I can't make it. I have a business meeting at one o'clock."

Flashing a sly smile, he lowered his mouth and kissed the corners of her lips. "I'm sure Becca won't mind if you reschedule. Tell her I wouldn't take no for an answer."

"I'm not having lunch with Becca. I'm meeting R.J. Johnson at Prime 112."

Ashton bolted upright in his chair. "R.J. Johnson?"

"Yes, do you know him?"

"Of course," he said with a shrug. "He owns practically everything in this town. Restaurants, bars and even gas stations."

"Best of all, he's a philanthropist with *really* deep pockets, and the foundation could use his generosity now more than ever."

"And you think it's wise to meet him at Prime 112?"

His sharp tone surprised her. "Yes, why not?"

"Because it's located inside a fancy boutique hotel."

"I didn't choose the restaurant, R.J. did. And to be honest it doesn't matter to me. All I care about is securing his financial support for the foundation—"

"He's married," Ashton blurted out, cutting her off. "His wife has health issues, so she doesn't venture out much anymore, but they live together on Fisher Island."

Confused, she stared blankly. She heard her cell phone ringing, suspected it was her mom finally returning her call, but decided to let her voice mail take the message. Haley didn't like what Ashton was implying, and wanted him to explain himself. "I'm sorry to hear about Mrs. Johnson's health issues, but what does that have to do with me?"

"R.J. is trouble. Stay away from him."

"I appreciate your concern, but I'm a big girl. I know what I'm doing."

"No, you don't. You have no idea what you're getting yourself into. R.J.'s favorite pastime is bedding and seducing young women, and I don't want you to fall in his trap,"

Ashton explained. “He’s twice your age, and a pro at luring females into bed.”

“I’m not looking for a father figure, or a sugar daddy, but thanks for the heads-up.”

“Haley, I’m serious.”

“So am I,” she shot back, determined to stand her ground. “Stay out of it, Ashton. My business affairs on behalf of The Aunt Penny Foundation don’t concern you.”

“I don’t want you to have lunch with him.”

The door opened, and a security guard with tattooed biceps marched inside. He took one look at them, spun on his heels and left the room. The guard left so quickly Haley knew he’d seen the don’t-mess-with-me expression on her face, and had decided to run for his life.

“Do you know how hard it was for me to get R.J. on the phone? I must have called his office a hundred times, and it took me another twenty minutes to convince him to meet with me.”

“You’re making a huge mistake. Cancel.”

“Don’t tell me what to do,” she snapped, losing her patience. “You’re not the boss of me, and there’s nothing you can say to change my mind, so quit badgering me.”

His laughter was loud and bitter. “Is that what you think I’m doing?”

If the shoe fit, she thought sourly, folding her arms across her chest. “How would you feel if I got mad at you because you were having a business dinner with an attractive woman?”

“It’s different,” he argued.

“Why? Because I’m a stupid, naïve woman who needs saving?”

Shaking his head, Ashton made a T with his hands, signaling for a timeout. “Hold on. I never said that. I trust you,

Haley. It's R.J. I don't trust. He tells tall tales, and I don't want you to be his next victim."

Ashton touched her arm, but Haley pulled it back. "I won't be. I know how to handle guys like R.J. He won't get the best of me."

"It doesn't matter what happens tomorrow. He'll tell his friends and associates you slept together and I don't want him to ruin your reputation."

The air was so thick with tension it was hard to breathe, but Haley spoke her mind. "It's a chance I'm willing to take. The Aunt Penny Foundation is drowning in debt, and his donation can help keep us afloat until the Millionaire Moguls party at the end of the month."

"How much money do you need? How much is R.J. giving you?"

Dropping her hands to her sides, Haley took a deep, calming breath. To make him understand the situation, Haley told Ashton about the bounced check, her conversation with the foundation's accountant days earlier and the dismal financial reports on her desk. "Three years ago, Becca got a financial commitment from her parents to help get The Aunt Penny Foundation off the ground, but after several years of the shaky economy the foundation is now facing a financial crisis, and I'll do anything to save it."

Wearing a sympathetic expression on his face, Ashton picked up his cell phone from off the counter and began typing. "This will only take a minute."

"Ashton, what are you doing?" In her peripheral vision, she noticed fans heading for the exits and glanced at the scoreboard. The game was over, but Haley was annoyed with Ashton, and she wanted to clear the air before he took her home.

"There, it's done." He pocketed his cell phone. "The email transfer went through."

Before she could question him, her cell buzzed, and Ashton gestured for her to pick it up. Noticing she had a new work email, Haley opened it. The message was from Ashton. He'd made a donation to The Aunt Penny Foundation seconds earlier, and when Haley saw the amount of his contribution she gasped. *OMG!*

Filled with mixed emotions Haley didn't know what to think. Couldn't speak.

"Now, all your problems are solved..."

The concierge returned to collect their plates, and Ashton trailed off. Glad for the interruption, Haley picked up her glass and sipped her mineral water. Damn. Why was Ashton trying to control her? Didn't he know it was a turn-off? A deal breaker? As much as Haley liked him, she loved her independence and would never date a guy who disrespected her—not even one worth millions.

"On behalf of The Aunt Penny Foundation, thank you for your very generous donation," she said tightly, forcing the words from her mouth. "I'll have someone in the finance department mail out your tax receipt first thing Monday morning."

His eyes narrowed. "What's wrong? Why are you mad?"

Haley didn't want to argue with Ashton, especially after he'd given the foundation a six-figure donation, but she had to be honest about her feelings. "Contrary to what you think, I can handle myself, and I won't let R.J. Johnson, or anyone else, take advantage of me"

"Understood, and for the record, I wasn't trying to control you. I just wanted to help."

Noticing the time on her watch, Haley tucked her clutch purse under her arm and rose to her feet. "We should go. Tomorrow's going to be a busy day, and we both need our rest."

"You're right." Standing, he wrapped an arm around her slim waist. "The Firebirds let me down tonight, but

I'm stoked you'll be at my polo match tomorrow cheering me on."

"Ashton, I'm not canceling my meeting. That would be rude and unprofessional."

His eyes widened with alarm, as if he'd come face-to-face with an ax-wielding madman. His jaw dropped, and his hands fell to his side. Ashton didn't speak, but his confusion and disappointment were evident. Hanging his head, he shoved his hands into his pockets. "I see."

To smooth things over, Haley extended an olive branch. "If you're not busy on Sunday night, I'd love to have you over for dinner. I'm making beef short ribs, sweet potatoes, collard greens and raspberry cheesecake for dessert."

His smile returned. "Thanks for the invitation. I'd love to come. What should I bring?"

"Surprise me."

Taking her hand, Ashton led Haley through the suite and out the door.

"I better take you home. It's getting late, and I'd hate for you to sleep in and miss your meeting tomorrow morning."

Swallowing a laugh, she stuck out her tongue. "Liar! That's *exactly* what you want."

"Don't blame me for wanting to spend all of my free time with you. It's not my fault you're a captivating beauty with a loveable personality."

His eyes smiled, and just like that her anger abated and her good mood returned.

"I didn't mean to upset you, and I'm sorry for snapping at you earlier. Am I forgiven?"

To make him laugh, she nodded. "But don't let it happen again, or it'll be the last thing you do!"

Ashton chuckled. "Duly noted. I'll be on my best behavior from here on out."

Chapter 8

"What's up, boss man?" Elijah Spear, a senior director of engineering at Rollins Aeronautics, entered Ashton's office, wearing a broad smile. "I haven't seen you all day. Where have you been hiding?"

Ashton glanced up from the financial report he was reading at his treadmill desk, and dropped his pen on the file. Walking at a leisurely pace, he noted the time on his computer and pressed the stop button. His desk had everything he needed—a laptop, phone, easel and paper trays—and since he'd started using it last year his productivity had increased.

"I've been around. I came by your office at lunchtime, but you were out."

The grin slid off Elijah's face. "I went to Lamaze class with the wife."

"How did it go?"

"Don't ask," he said in a somber tone of voice. His royal blue suit jacket, matching dress pants and tropical-print shirt screamed Miami, but Elijah was born and raised on a reservation in South Dakota, and he was proud of his Native American roots. "I saw things on that birthing video no man should ever see, and I don't know if I'll ever recover."

Ashton picked up his water bottle and took a long drink. He'd spent the morning in meetings, discussing ways to boost company morale and strategizing about how to reduce cost and increase profits. At noon, he'd left the office and driven the thirty miles to their Fort Lauderdale plant. Touching base with employees and inspecting the new and improved safety features implemented last month had taken several hours, but the visit had been worthwhile. His father preferred delegating tasks to department managers, but Ashton liked to "feel" what was happening at the company, and he visited the plant three times a week.

"Can I catch a ride with you to the country club?" Elijah asked. "My Beemer's in the shop again, so I need a lift. I figured we could discuss the German deal on the drive over."

Every Friday, after work, the senior management team went to the Miami Country Club for dinner and drinks, but Ashton wasn't joining them tonight. He had big plans with Haley, and he'd been looking forward to their date at Cipriani Downtown Miami all day.

Just the thought of her warmed him all over. Despite their busy work schedules, they'd seen each other every day since the Firebirds game two weeks earlier. Ashton used to spend his weekends relaxing at home, playing online chess and working in his home office, but these days, Haley—not Rollins Aeronautics—was his focus. She was personable and down-to-earth, not a diva stuck on material things, and he loved being with her. They did yoga in his home gym, explored museums and art galleries on rainy days, went to movie premieres and amusement parks. It didn't matter what they did—Haley made their dates fun and exciting.

"Elijah, count me out. I have plans."

"All work and no play makes Ashton a dull boy," he joked.

The engineer was a rabid sports fan who loved golf more than a PGA champion, and if not for his commitment to Rollins Aeronautics he'd spend all his time at the Miami Country Club perfecting his golf swing, or at the beach surfing. Happily married, with two sons and another kid on the way, Elijah was not only his employee but a good friend.

"We better hurry," Elijah said, ignoring Ashton's comment. "If we're late, the guys will make us pick up the tab again, and I hate spending money, unless it's on my 78 Chevy. You feel me?"

"Elijah, I'm serious. I'm not going."

"Do you ever do anything besides work?"

"As a matter of fact I do," Ashton said with a wide grin. "I romance my girl."

"Your girl?" Entering the office, Elijah barked a laugh, shaking his head as if he didn't believe what he was hearing. "Tell me more."

"Her name's Haley Adams, and she's the CEO of a non-profit organization."

Elijah dropped down on one of the leather chairs. "Now everything makes sense."

Ashton picked up his towel and wiped his sweaty face. "What makes sense?"

"You've been Mr. Happy-Go-Lucky for the past couple weeks, and I couldn't figure out why, but it's obvious this Haley chick pulled you out of your miserable funk!" Leaning forward in his chair, he rested his palms on the desk and spoke in a loud, animated voice. "Who is she?

What does she look like? Shoot, if you're claiming her she must be a ten!"

Ashton didn't want to discuss Haley with anyone—not his parents or his friends and colleagues—but Elijah was so happy for him he couldn't resist bragging about his smart, successful girlfriend. "Haley's the real deal, the total package, and I want to settle down with her."

"You can tell me more about Haley during our flight to Caracas tomorrow," Elijah said with a toothy smile. "What time should I be at the airport?"

"Nice try, Elijah, but you're still not going."

"Come on, man, you need me. Who's going to keep you company at the hotel? Who's going to join you for dinner? And who's going to be your wingman at the club?"

"Elijah, you have to work this weekend, and furthermore your wife would never forgive you if you were traveling and missed the birth of your third child."

Dismissing Ashton's words with a flick of his hand, Elijah crossed his legs at the ankles. "You've seen one water birth, you've seen them all!"

The engineer gave a hearty laugh, but Ashton knew Elijah loved his children dearly and wouldn't trade his family for anything in the world.

"You have to bring me with you."

Ashton raised an eyebrow. "Why?"

"Because I love Venezuela. I know all of the best places to eat, surf and party," Elijah explained, rubbing his hands together. "Come on. Let me come. You won't regret it."

Ashton gave some thought to what Elijah said. His friend was right. He shouldn't go to Venezuela alone. He should invite someone lively and spontaneous and fun who loved trying new things. *Haley.* Thrilled about the prospect of spending the weekend with her in his favorite city, Ashton considered what it would take to convince her to join him in Caracas.

Elijah gave it one more try. "Traveling alone sucks, so if I were you I'd take me up on my very generous offer."

"Who told you I'm traveling alone?"

Surprise flashed in his eyes. "You're taking your girl to Venezuela? Why?"

"Because she's important to me, and I enjoy her company."

"Big mistake. Don't do it. People will think you're sprung."

Shrugging, Ashton tossed his towel down on the desk. "I don't care what people think. Haley's my girl, and there's no one else I'd rather travel with than her."

His desk phone buzzed, and Mrs. Vaughn's small, thin voice filled the office. In her sixties, with decades of experience in the engineering field under her belt, the grandmother of six was the best secretary he'd ever had, and Ashton paid her well to ensure none of his competitors stole her away. "Yes, Mrs. Vaughn, what is it?"

"Joshua DeLong is on line one again. Do you wish to take his call at this time?"

Gripping the receiver, he spoke through clenched teeth. "Tell him I'm busy."

"I told him that when he phoned this morning."

"Nothing's changed," he said, fed up with the incessant calls. "Just get rid of him."

"Very well, sir. Is there anything you need me to do before I leave for the day?"

"No, have fun at the opera." He softened his tone. "Give your husband my regards. I heard Mozart's *Cosi Fan Tutte* is a bore, but you're definitely worth the trouble."

Mrs. Vaughn laughed. "I most certainly am!"

Dropping the phone on the cradle, Ashton expelled a

deep breath. All week, Joshua had been blowing up his phone, and all week he'd been dodging his calls. Worse still, he'd asked Haley to speak to him on his behalf, which led to them arguing in his Corvette last night. Ashton didn't care that Joshua had a long list of connections. He was a nuisance, a thorn in his side, and at the next Prescott George meeting he'd tell him just that. The organization was supposed to be a brotherhood, tighter than a fraternity, and Joshua was destroying their bond. He had to go, and not a moment too soon.

Ashton considered reaching out to Daniel, but struck the idea from his mind. Since college, they'd been enemies and ten years later nothing had changed. Back in the day, Daniel had tried sabotaging his relationship with Mia, and Ashton knew the real estate mogul still blamed him for her death. They rarely spoke, and when they did it was only at Millionaire Moguls meetings, and even then it was like pulling teeth. No, he'd just have to handle Joshua himself.

Elijah's voice broke into his thoughts. "Do you want to be my partner for the golf tournament in December? You don't need the fifty-thousand-dollar cash prize, but I sure could use it." Wearing a pensive expression on his face, he gazed out the floor-to-ceiling window. "With another baby on the way, and Yindi off work for the next six months, money is tighter than ever."

As much as Ashton liked shooting the breeze with Elijah, he had to get going. He'd planned to go home to change out of his suit, and into his favorite jeans, but now he had no choice but to shower and change in his office bathroom. Busy doing paperwork and joking around with Elijah, he'd lost track of time, and if he didn't leave in the next ten minutes he'd be late to meet Haley. And he couldn't risk screwing up again.

His thoughts returned to last weekend. On Saturday, he'd arrived at Discovery Park five minutes late and was shocked to find Haley shooting hoops with an all-male team of college students. Haley's radiant smile and bubbly personality drew people to her, and Ashton couldn't take her anywhere without guys flirting with her. He tried not to get angry, knew he'd lose her if he was jealous and controlling, but it was hard to stand by and watch men ogle his girlfriend. It took ten minutes for Haley to say her goodbyes, and by that time all of the players had promised to volunteer at the soup kitchen. It took everything in him not to curse, but he'd smiled politely and hustled her to their secluded picnic spot across the field before she could hand out her business cards.

"You better hurry or you'll miss your ride to the country club," he told Elijah.

"Have fun in Venezuela. Don't do anything I wouldn't do."

"I most certainly will." Grabbing his files, he stepped off the treadmill. "I'm taking my girl with me, and we're going to have an incredible trip."

Elijah clapped him on the back. "Dude, stop. You're gushing like a water fountain!"

Instead of feeling embarrassed, Ashton felt proud. He'd found the woman of his dreams, and he was going to show her what she meant to him, but first he had to persuade her to accompany him to Venezuela. And he would.

"I'll see you on Tuesday. Good luck with Lamaze class."

"Bye, boss man. Have a safe flight."

Elijah left, and Ashton sprung into action. Making a mental checklist of everything he needed for his trip to Caracas, he tossed the files and folders into his Louis Vuitton satchel and slammed it shut. Whistling his favorite jazz song, he selected an outfit from his wardrobe and strode into the bathroom, feeling on top of the world. Now that he had Haley in his life, he had everything a man could want, and Ashton wasn't traveling to Venezuela without her.

Chapter 9

Cipriani Downtown Miami was a place to see and be seen, but Ashton was more interested in Haley than the A-list celebrities dining nearby with their massive entourages. In her teal cocktail dress, teardrop earrings and a colorful beaded necklace, she looked as regal as the first lady, and Ashton couldn't take his eyes off her. Or keep his hands to himself.

Reaching across the table, Ashton touched her smooth, soft flesh, caressing her wrist with his fingertips. He wished they were at his estate, making out on his couch again, instead of at Cipriani. At home, he wouldn't have to hold back. He could kiss her until he'd had his fill of her. Though Ashton knew that was impossible. He could never get enough of her.

"Are you sure you're the CEO of a nonprofit organization and not a model? Because you look like you just came from a photo shoot," Ashton said, squeezing her hand.

Laughing, Haley admonished him to quit teasing her. "Don't make fun."

"I'm not. That dress was made for you. From the moment we entered the restaurant men *and* women have been watching you, and I don't blame them."

"They're staring because I'm having dinner with the most eligible bachelor in the city."

"I'm not a bachelor anymore. I'm your man, Haley, and proud of it. You're a gentle, compassionate soul, and I cherish every moment we spend together."

"Are you sure you're the COO of an aeronautical company and not a poet, because you sure sound like one," she joked, winking at him.

Hearing applause, Ashton glanced around the main-floor dining room. A gentleman with silver hair was on bended knee, and a dark-skinned woman in a strapless, metallic gown had tears in her eyes. It was a heartwarming scene, and Ashton couldn't help but wonder what Haley's reaction would be if he popped the question.

"This restaurant is amazing," Haley said. "How did you find it?"

"Through one of the moguls. Daniel Cobb knows the best places to eat, and he was bang-on about Cipriani. Everything's exceptional. The food, the service, the ambience."

"I agree. I feel like I'm *actually* in Italy!" Laughing, Haley forked a piece of veal into her mouth and closed her eyes. "Wow, this is so good."

"I'm glad you're enjoying yourself."

"I am. It's my first time here, but it definitely won't be my last."

Pleased, Ashton nodded in agreement. Bright and airy, with chic white-and-blue décor and high ceilings, the restaurant offered panoramic views of Biscayne Bay, an eclectic menu rich with creativity and flavor, and a vibrant atmosphere.

Italian music was playing, and animated laughter and conversation filled the air. Cipriani was legendary in Miami, and one of Ashton's favorite restaurants. It was only blocks away from Rollins Aeronautics. Ashton ate there several times a week and was never disappointed.

Picking up his flute, Ashton surveyed all of the food on the table in their cozy corner booth. The appetizer platter was plentiful and delicious and the Bolognese was the best dish he'd ever tasted.

"Miss, did you enjoy your meal?"

Ashton was annoyed, but he hid his frustration. The waiter was back. Again. For the second time in minutes. To flirt with Haley, no doubt. He was a slim, bearded man with a thick Italian accent, and annoying as hell. The waiter stared at Haley with stars in his eyes, as if she was the only person in the room, and Ashton didn't like it.

"Luigi, you were right! The spices in the veal are remarkable," she said, an awestruck expression on her face. "And the ricotta ravioli is out of this world!"

A broad grin covered his mouth. "I'm thrilled that you enjoyed your meal. Can I interest you in something from the dessert menu?"

"Come back later," Ashton said with a polite smile. "I want to discuss something important with my *girlfriend*, and we can't be interrupted."

Nodding, the waiter picked up the empty dishes and hurried to the kitchen.

Ashton draped an arm around her bare shoulders. "I want to see you tomorrow," he whispered in her hair, inhaling her scent. "Please say yes."

"What do you have in mind?"

"Dinner, dancing and sightseeing in Venezuela. Are you interested?"

"Oh, that's right, you're going to Caracas this weekend

to speak at the Caracas Business Summit. You must be so excited."

"I'd be excited if you were accompanying me on the trip." Ashton kissed her cheek. "Nothing beats a romantic weekend in Caracas."

He held his breath, hoped she'd accept his invitation.

"I'd love to come."

Ashton wanted to pump his fist in the air, but restrained himself from cheering. He stared deep into her eyes, and knew without a doubt that Haley shared his feelings. Not caring that they were at a fancy restaurant, he made his move.

Leaning into her, he captured her lips in a kiss. It was perfect. *She* was perfect. And the longer they kissed the more Ashton craved her. Wanted her. Needed her. Wished they were alone at his estate, in his bed. His hands slid under the table and caressed her thighs. He never knew it could be like this, never imagined he'd meet a woman who'd capture his heart. Now that Ashton had Haley he had everything he'd ever wanted in life.

Feasting on her lips, an erection rising in his pants, Ashton tried to remember the last time he'd had sex. Three months? Six? Nine? He had needs, and right now he needed Haley in his bed. They were exclusive, and Ashton didn't want anyone else, but he remembered the conversation they'd had weeks earlier about her celibacy and dropped his hands to his sides.

"Ashton, honey, is that you?"

Ashton froze. Hearing his mother's voice, he pulled away from Haley and opened his eyes. Damn. He hadn't imagined it. Wasn't dreaming. Seeing his mother at Cipriani was a shock, but there she was. Dressed in a colorful scarf and a stylish burgundy pantsuit, Joan Rollins flounced into the dining room, frantically waving her bejeweled hands.

For two weeks, he'd successfully dodged his mother, but now there was nowhere to hide. No escape route. Nothing he could do to avoid her. So much for keeping his relationship with Haley a secret, he thought, picking up his glass and guzzling the rest of his ice water.

Alexander appeared at Joan's side, and Ashton knew the Man upstairs had it out for him. "Mom, Dad, what are you doing here?"

"We have to eat, too," Alexander said, taking off his sunglasses.

His dad's smile was forced, and his tone was so cold Ashton wished he was wearing a winter jacket. Ignoring his father, he stood and kissed his mother on the cheek. Joan held him tight, rocking him from side to side, and he had no choice but to hug her back.

"Honey, it's great to see you. What a pleasant surprise."

Ashton coughed into his fist. He'd planned to introduce Haley to his parents at the Prescott George anniversary party, not tonight at his favorite restaurant, but now he had no choice but to come clean to his mom and dad about his love life.

"We'd love to meet your date, so don't keep us in suspense," Joan said. "Who is she?"

Heat flooded his body. Ashton couldn't remember ever seeing his mother giddy, and he hoped she didn't do anything to embarrass him, like break out his baby pictures or gush about him being the "perfect" son. Ashton didn't have to worry about his dad. Alexander looked annoyed, and Ashton suspected his mom had dragged his dad out of the house again. The consummate trophy wife, Joan loved to socialize and mingle.

"Mom, Dad, this is my girlfriend, Haley Adams."

Joan rested a hand on her chest. "Your what?"

Now Ashton had his dad's full attention. His father

stared at him as if he'd taken leave of his senses, and his mouth was open so wide Ashton could practically see his wisdom teeth. He was proud to have Haley in his life, and he wanted his family to know she was special to him. And if Alexander didn't like it, tough. Screw him. This time his dad wasn't calling the shots. He was.

Rising to her feet, Haley straightened her dress and offered her hand in greeting. "It's a pleasure to meet you both," she said brightly, her cheery voice conveying her happiness. "Ashton's told me a lot about you, but he failed to mention what a beautiful couple you are. Now I know where he got his good looks from."

"Why, thank you, Haley. What a kind thing to say." Beaming, Joan fingered the diamond pendant on her necklace. "By any chance, are you related to the Adams family of Fisher Island? I've never met them, but I'm a huge fan of their company, Organic Life."

"No, I'm not."

Joan gestured to the booth. "Is it okay if we join you? Our party hasn't arrived yet, and it would be swell to get to know Haley better, don't you agree, Alexander?"

No! Ashton shouted inwardly. "Mom, we were just leaving. Maybe next time."

"Nonsense. Surely you can visit with your parents for a few minutes."

"I wish we could, but we have to get going."

"I was in labor with you for twenty hours, seventeen minutes and fifty-three seconds," Joan reminded him, flinging her pashmina scarf over her shoulders. "And I think you owe it to your long-suffering parents to spend a few minutes with them."

The matter decided, Alexander and Joan sat down in the booth.

"How did you two kids meet?" Joan asked.

"Haley is the founder and CEO of The Aunt Penny Foundation, and we met at a Prescott George function," Ashton explained. "The Moguls will be presenting her organization with a large donation at the anniversary party at the end of the month."

The waiter arrived, offering drinks, but Mr. and Mrs. Rollins declined.

"You're an articulate, accomplished young woman, Ms. Adams. It's no wonder my son is smitten with you." Alexander's words were kind, but he wore a somber expression on his face. "If you don't mind me asking, what do your parents do for a living?"

Ashton glared at his dad, but before he could speak, Haley answered the question.

"My mother works as a cook at a hospital cafeteria in Pensacola, and my father is a sanitation worker. My parents divorced when I was a teenager, but we're still a close family and I wouldn't be the woman I am today without their love and guidance."

Alexander nodded, and Ashton could tell his father was impressed by her response.

"Tell us more about your formative years. Were you born and raised in Miami?"

To his surprise, Haley looked amused, not annoyed by his father's questions, and listening to her brought a grin to Ashton's mouth. She answered all of his parents' questions with poise and wit, even joking about her humble beginnings and her undying love of Stevie Wonder.

"They're here!" Rising to her feet, Joan fluffed her short, black curls and tucked her beaded clutch purse under her arm. "I wish we could visit longer, but the Ellingtons just arrived, and I want to hear all about their vacation in Tofino with the Clooneys."

There is *a God!* Ashton thought, with a sigh of relief.

Five more minutes with his dad, and he probably would have lost his temper. It didn't matter where Haley was from, or what her parents did for a living. At least not to him. She was special, someone he could picture himself building a life with, and Ashton wasn't going to let his father ruin their relationship.

Joan kissed Haley on each cheek. "We look forward to seeing you at the Prescott George anniversary party," she said in a breezy tone of voice. "You'll sit at our table."

"Thank you, Mrs. Rollins, for the very generous offer. I'd like that."

"Have a safe trip to Caracas." Alexander stood and adjusted his gray tie. "Call me after the conference. I want to hear about the contacts you made, and any follow-up meetings."

Ashton pressed his lips together. It was on the tip of his tongue to boast, to tell his parents Haley was accompanying him to Venezuela, but since he didn't want them to be all up in his business he nodded in response to his father's request. "Will do. Have a good night."

His parents left, and Ashton blew out a deep breath. "Baby, sorry about that," he said with an apologetic smile. "If I'd known my parents would be at Cipriani tonight I would've picked a restaurant clear across town!"

"Ashton, they're an adorable couple, and I'm glad I had the chance to meet them."

"We better get out of here before they come back," he joked.

The waiter returned, and as expected his gaze landed on Haley. "Have you decided on dessert?" he asked, clasping his hands behind his back like a dutiful servant. "Everything in the menu is exquisite, but the chocolate pistachio tartufo is my favorite."

Ashton opened his wallet, took out his platinum credit

card and placed it on the table. "Just the check, please. Thanks."

"Very well, sir. It's been my pleasure to serve you both."

Seconds later, after he'd paid the bill, Ashton hustled Haley through the dining room and out the door. It was early evening but the sky was still bright with sunshine, and a light breeze was blowing along Brickell Avenue. The street was lined with restaurants, Fortune 500 companies, high-end boutiques and condominiums, and everywhere Ashton looked he saw well-dressed people. "I hope you're not tired, because the night's still young."

Leading her over to his Rolls-Royce Phantom, which was parked across the street under a lamp post, he affectionately patted her hips. "If we hurry, we can catch Rashad J's performance at The Stage. He did an hour-long set last night, and I heard it was outstanding."

"Maybe next time. I still have to do laundry tonight and pack for our trip."

"Don't sweat it. I'll buy you everything you need in Caracas."

"Thanks, but no thanks," she said, fervently shaking her head. "Besides, you need to save your money for the Prescott George anniversary party. It's the social event of the year, and your wealthy, esteemed guests are expecting you to wow them, so you better deliver!"

Ashton chuckled. Stopping at the intersection, he wrapped Haley up in his arms and kissed the top of her head. Pop music blared from the bar across the street, and Haley swayed her body to the infectious beat. He loved the way she moved, and for the second time in minutes he couldn't help thinking about her—naked—in his bed.

"What time should I be at the airport in the morning?"

Blinking, he cleared the X-rated image from his mind. "I'll pick you up at eight a.m."

"No worries. I'll drive myself. That will be easier."

"And rob me the pleasure of your company during my commute? No way!"

"But you have to pass the airport to pick me up."

"You're worth the detour."

"Sure, sure," she quipped. "I bet you say that to all the women you travel with."

"I've never traveled with a girlfriend before. This is a first."

"Seriously? Wow, I feel honored."

Clasping her hand, Ashton led her across the street. Excited about their trip to Venezuela, he gazed at Haley with longing in his eyes. They were closer than ever, and there was no doubt in his mind that by the time they returned to Miami on Monday they'd be lovers.

Chapter 10

Seated comfortably in the backseat of the black Land Rover, staring out the open window, Haley still couldn't believe she was in Caracas, Venezuela, with Ashton. They'd flown there in the Rollins family jet, a gleaming 747 that seated forty people. When she'd boarded, and saw the gold décor throughout the cabin, the wood-paneled galley and the elegant guest quarters, a gasp had fallen from her lips. Feeling guilty about being on the fancy aircraft while her colleagues were hard at work at the office, Haley had tried to tamp down her excitement. But it was impossible. Especially when Ashton had fed her caviar and held her hand as they enjoyed their delicious meal.

On the three-hour flight, Ashton had worked on his speech, while she'd watched an old Pam Grier movie on her laptop. Upon arriving at the Simón Bolívar International Airport, they'd met Ashton's personal driver and bodyguard at the baggage claim, then had ducked into an SUV.

"You're so quiet," Ashton said, giving her a sideways

glance. Pocketing his cell phone, he took her hand in his and gave it a light squeeze. "Everything okay?"

"Yeah, I'm great. Just trying to take everything in."

As the armored car cruised through the streets, Haley marveled at the colorful houses and the towering skyscrapers in the vibrant, metropolitan city. Soaking in the ambience, she inhaled the heady fragrance in the air. Billboards lined the roads and merchants, shouting in Spanish, hawked their wares. The streets were filled with smartly dressed businessmen and hand-holding couples, and as they sped through the intersection Haley noticed children flying kites and dribbling soccer balls in a nearby park.

"Sir, there's a three-car pileup on Avenida Boyacá," the driver explained. "Do you still want to go to the hotel first, or should I take you directly to the business summit?"

Juan, the middle-aged driver, and Reynaldo, their personal bodyguard, looked like twins. Of Spanish descent, both men had brown eyes, dark hair and muscled biceps. They spoke perfect English and addressed Ashton with such reverence Haley knew they respected him.

"Take us to the hotel as planned," Ashton told Juan.

Tearing her gaze away from the window, Haley reached into her purse and took out her handkerchief. Boiling in her bohemian-style dress and gladiator sandals, she dabbed at the sweat on her forehead and neck. "What time do you have to be at the conference?"

"One o'clock. I'll see you to your suite, then leave."

"My suite? We're not sleeping together—?" Embarrassed by the slip of the tongue, Haley dropped her gaze to her lap and fiddled with her bracelet. "We're not sharing a suite?"

"No, we have separate, but adjoining rooms."

Haley didn't like the sound of that. What if Ashton met someone at the business summit that afternoon? Where would that leave her? He didn't strike her as a cheater or give off that bad-boy vibe, but still, doubts filled her mind. "That's no fun. What's the point of traveling together if you're going to be off doing your own thing?"

"I didn't invite you on this trip to lure you into bed."

Why not? Haley thought, shooting him an incredulous look behind her oval-shaped sunglasses. *Don't you know how much I want you? How much I desire you? Isn't it obvious?*

"I just want you to enjoy Caracas the way I do," Ashton said, "and experience all that it has to offer."

Ashton gave her a peck on the cheek, and Haley snuggled against him. Cuddling with him was her new favorite pastime, and being in his arms would never grow old. Feeling his hand caressing up and down her arm made her feel warm inside. Ashton never crossed the line or pressured her for sex, which only made Haley want him even more.

"I wish we could have lunch together, but I'm pressed for time."

"Ashton, you don't have to escort me to my suite. I can find it myself."

"I know, but my mother raised me to be a gentleman, and Joan would kick my ass up and down Fisher Island Road if she knew I wasn't treating you like the queen that you are."

They kissed, and Haley melted into his arms. She'd never told a man she loved him, had never felt compelled to before today, but the words were on the tip of her tongue. Worried she'd scare him off if she confessed the truth, Haley struck the thought from her mind.

Thirty minutes later, the car stopped in front of Cayena Caracas. Moving swiftly, Reynaldo opened the back door and retrieved the luggage from the trunk. Ashton clasped Haley's hand and led her inside the sleek, ultramodern building overlooking El Ávila Mountain.

Taking off her sunglasses, Haley gawked at the sun-drenched lobby. Located in the most exclusive area of Caracas, the boutique hotel had everything a traveler could want. Fine restaurants, a fitness center, a rooftop pool all designed with luxury and comfort in mind. Pristine and beautiful, with designer furniture and Venezuelan art, the hotel embodied sophistication and glamour. The aroma of coffee and tropical fruit pervaded the air, tickling Haley's nose, and she licked her lips.

"Mr. Rollins, how wonderful to see you again. Welcome back to Cayena Caracas!"

Instinctively, Haley tightened her hold on his forearm. Everyone in the lobby was staring at them, and she knew it was because of Ashton's impressive stature. He emitted wealth and power, and they couldn't go anywhere without women making eyes at him.

"Gracias, Mariana. Es muy bueno estar de vuelta."

As Ashton spoke to the buxom hotel clerk in Spanish, Haley stared at him, enthralled by the dreamy sound of his voice. Another female clerk appeared at the counter, then two more, and they chatted and laughed with Ashton as if they were his friends.

"I didn't know you spoke Spanish," Haley said as he led her through the lobby with his driver and bodyguard in tow. It was weird having security follow them around, but since Ashton said it was necessary she didn't argue with him. "How did you learn the language?"

"In Spain. My parents sent me there for the summer when I was sixteen, and I quickly picked up the language. Once I mastered it, it was easy to learn Italian and Portuguese."

"Wow, you're good at everything. Must be nice."

"Not everything. I suck at dating." Ashton wore a boyish smile. "I've been on more dates than *The Bachelor*, and according to my mom I get an F in relationships."

"I find that hard to believe. You're such a catch."

"I am?"

Scoffing, Haley rolled her eyes. "Oh, stop," she said, playfully swatting his shoulder. "You and I both know you have hundreds of female admirers."

Ashton looked pained, not proud, and slowly shook his head. "Haley, that's not true."

"Yes it is. Just look around. Everyone wants a piece of you."

"Yeah, but for all the wrong reasons."

"You expect me to believe you're not flattered by all the attention? Most men would kill to have women proposition them on a daily basis, so what makes you different?"

"I've never been that guy. I want one special woman in my life who loves me for me and not because of my last name or because of my wealth."

They boarded the elevator alone, and Haley was grateful to have Ashton to herself for a few precious minutes. After weeks of dating, he was finally opening up to her, and Haley wanted to hear more. He sounded bitter, unlike his calm, cool self, and she wanted to know why.

"Don't get me wrong," he continued, as if peeking into her mind and reading her thoughts. "I'm not complaining. It's great to have money, but contrary to what people think, my life hasn't been a walk in the park. I never know if someone likes me for me, or because of what they think I can do for them. It's hard for me to let people into my world."

Moved by his words, Haley smiled with sympathy.

"My friends think I have it all, but success means nothing if you have no one to share it with." Ashton locked eyes with her. "And, Haley, I want that person to be you."

If the elevator doors didn't slide open, and a family of five wasn't standing in the hallway, Haley would have kissed him. They had an audience, though, and since she didn't want to give the children an eyeful she stepped off the elevator and searched for her room.

YOUR PARTICIPATION IS REQUESTED!

Dear Reader,

Since you are a lover of our books – we would like to get to know you!

Inside you will find a short Reader's Survey. Sharing your answers with us will help our editorial staff understand who you are and what activities you enjoy.

To thank you for your participation, we would like to send you 2 books and 2 gifts – **ABSOLUTELY FREE!**

Enjoy your gifts with our appreciation,

Pam Powers

SEE INSIDE FOR READER'S SURVEY

Finding suite 220, Haley took out her key card.

"Allow me." Ashton plucked the card out of her hand, slid it inside the lock, then threw open the door. Stepping aside, he bowed chivalrously at the waist. *"Bienvenidos, Senorita Adams!"*

As she entered the suite, Haley's eyes fell upon the floor-to-ceiling windows. Sunshine spilled into the room, inundating the space with warmth and light. A vase filled with colorful tulips sat on the mahogany desk. Haley loved everything about the suite—the four-poster bed, the crystal reading lamps, the plush rugs and silk drapes—and she took pictures of her opulent digs to send to Becca.

"What do you think?"

"I think I'm going to quit my job and relocate to Cayena Caracas!"

Ashton chuckled. "Once I return from the summit I'm all yours. We'll have dinner at the best restaurant in the city and take in a salsa performance at Centro Cultural Chacao."

"Don't rush back on my account. I have plenty to do while you're gone."

"You do? Like what?"

Haley reached into her purse, took out her Venezuela travel guide and skimmed chapter one. "I'm going to Centro de Arte Los Galpones, La Praline Chocolatier to buy cacao chocolate tins for Becca and Aunt Penny, and to the open-air market at Plaza Caracas."

"Wait until I get back. We'll go together."

"What do you expect me to do for the next five hours? Twiddle my thumbs?"

"No, of course not. Watch a movie, grab a late lunch in the on-site restaurant or check out the rooftop pool."

"Ashton, I didn't come to Caracas to hang out at the hotel all day."

"Not all day. Just until I get back this afternoon."

"Why?" she argued. "I'm perfectly capable of going out alone. I do it all the time. Furthermore, I enjoy my own company. I'm the bomb!"

Her joke fell flat, and Ashton folded his arms rigidly across his chest.

"Haley, this isn't Miami."

"I'm well aware of that, but I'm not a kid. I'm a seasoned traveler," she explained, annoyed with his curt tone and caveman attitude. "After I graduated from university, I traveled alone throughout Europe, without a single mishap. I know what to do to be safe. I'll be fine."

"If you insist on venturing out, take a taxi. I don't like the idea of you wandering the streets alone, so I'll arrange transportation with the front desk before I leave."

"Ashton, I'm not a child. I know what's best for me, not you."

"I don't want to argue about this."

"Then don't tell me what to do," she snapped. Ashton wasn't happy unless he was calling the shots, and that didn't sit well with her. His controlling ways were a turn-off, and if he didn't stop ordering her around she was getting on the first flight back to Miami.

His cell phone rang, but Ashton didn't answer it.

"Do you always have to have your own way?" he asked her instead.

A stinging resort was on the tip of her tongue, but Haley clamped her lips together to trap it inside. The last thing she wanted to do was argue with him, so she forced a smile and wisely changed the subject. "Have fun at the conference. I'll see you later."

"Are you sure you don't want to come? The Caracas Business Summit attracts powerful and influential people, and it's one of the best conferences I've ever been to."

"Thanks, but no thanks. I have plenty to see and do this afternoon."

"Remember what I said."

"Don't worry. I'll take the bellman with me," she joked, hoping to lighten the tense mood. "He's young, tall and athletic. I'm sure I'll be perfectly safe *and* highly entertained."

Ashton wagged a finger in her face. "Hey, you're mine. No fraternizing with the help!"

His laughter warmed her all over, and the feel of his hands stroking her hips had a calming effect on her mood. His touch made her frustration abate and her spirits brighten. "I'll be good, Ashton. I promise. Don't worry about me."

"That's my girl."

His words gave her a rush, causing her skin to tingle with goose bumps.

"Be dressed and ready to go by six o'clock," he instructed, brushing his fingertips against her cheeks. "And wear something that shows off your sensational legs."

"Yes, sir," she said with a nod. "I will. With pleasure."

Halcy expected Ashton to leave, but he pulled her into his arms and hugged her tight, as if he had all the time in the world to play and cuddle.

"I want to kiss you, but I'm worried if I do I'll never leave this suite."

"It's a good thing I have enough self-control for the both of us, isn't it?"

Closing her eyes, Haley kissed Ashton with such longing and passion his knees buckled, and they tumbled onto the satin-draped bed in a tangled heap.

Haley paid the taxi driver, thanked him for the ride and exited the vehicle in front of the open-air market at Plaza Caracas. Wanting to buy a gift for Ashton, Haley hoped she'd be able to find something special for him and made a mental note to also purchase a thank-you card as well.

Remembering their afternoon make-out session in her suite made her skin flush with heat and her nipples harden under her yellow tank top. It had taken every ounce of self-control she had, but after rolling around with Ashton on the bed for several minutes, she'd dragged him to his feet and ushered him out the door.

An hour later, freshly showered and changed, she'd hailed a cab to take her to Centro de Arte Los Galpones. It had a charming art gallery teeming with restaurants with authentic Venezuelan cuisine. At Tolón Fashion Mall, she'd purchased cookie tins for her hardworking employees at the foundation. And, once she bought something for Ashton she would return to the hotel.

Hundreds of vendors were crammed into the space, selling everything from handmade crafts to fashion, electronics and food. Salsa music and boisterous laughter and conversation filled the crowded market, and Haley loved the lively atmosphere.

She licked her lips. The piquant aroma wafting through the air made her mouth water and her stomach rumble. Hungry and thirsty, she stopped in front of a food cart and purchased a snack. Made with tropical fruit, crushed ice and water, the *batido* was the perfect antidote for the stifling heat.

Holding her ice-cold drink in one hand and her bag of *tequeños* in the other, she decided life couldn't be any better. She couldn't imagine a more beautiful day, and everywhere she looked people were smiling and laughing. Haley missed Ashton and wondered how he was faring at his conference, but she enjoyed having some time to herself to shop and explore, without his bodyguards watching her every move.

Munching on the savory bread sticks, Haley strolled from one booth to the next, perusing the goods and chatting with friendly merchants. For hours, she tried on funky T-shirts and hats, sampled Venezuelan foods and snapped pictures with her phone. She bought a beaded purse for Sienna, several souvenirs for her parents and a bottle of Pampero rum for Calvin.

Guilt washed over Haley as she remembered the argument she'd had with the accountant days earlier during the monthly budget meeting. They'd butted heads over the finances again, and Haley hoped he'd accept her liquid peace offering.

Out of the corner of her eye, Haley caught sight of yoga-themed merchandise displayed in a corner stall and stopped in her tracks. Deciding it was perfect for Ashton, she purchased three copper sculptures, a card sure to make him laugh out loud and a set of mantra blocks. Pleased, Haley couldn't wait to see the look on his face when he opened the gift bag.

Haley checked her watch, saw the time and gasped. It was five-thirty. She should be back at the hotel, getting ready for her date, not searching for bargains. Speed-walking to the entrance of the plaza, Haley glanced up and down the street for a taxicab. Motorcycles zipped by at death-defying speeds, and although she wanted to return to the hotel before Ashton, she didn't feel like living on the edge, so she decided a motorcycle ride was out of the question.

Clouds obscured the sun, and rain drizzled down from the sky. Shielding her eyes with her hands, she searched around for somewhere to take cover. Haley didn't realize she was in trouble until it was too late. A short, heavyset man who reeked of onions appeared out of nowhere and grabbed her forearm.

"Dame tu bolso o en otro sitio," he hissed through crooked teeth. *"Rapido!"*

Fear churned inside her stomach. Haley didn't understand what he was saying, but his face was dark with anger, and he was holding her so tight a searing pain stabbed her arm. Terrified, Haley didn't know what to do to save herself. She wanted to scream, but her lips wouldn't move. Her pulse drummed inside her ears, making it impossible to think.

"Stupid American woman," he spat. "Give me your purse or I'll ruin your pretty face."

Like hell you will! Her hands curled into fists, and adrenaline surged through her veins. Never before had Haley felt such rage, and when the mugger tried to rip the bags from her hands Haley found her voice. "Let go of me!"

"Do you want to die?"

"Do you?" Something clicked inside her mind. Remembering the self-defense moves her father had taught her years earlier, Haley poked his eyes with her fingers, then thrust her knee in his groin. Wincing in pain, the crook cursed in Spanish and fell to the ground with a thud.

"Haley!"

Seeing Ashton up the block, Haley took off running down the street and threw herself into his open arms. Relief flooded her body. She was safe, and the mugger couldn't hurt her, but she couldn't stop shaking. "What are you doing here? How did you know where to find me?"

"I didn't, but I remembered the places you mentioned this morning, so when I returned to the hotel an hour ago and didn't see you, I decided to track you down," he explained, taking her shopping bags. "This was my last stop."

Frowning, Ashton glanced at the man on the ground, groaning and cursing in Spanish. "Did he hurt you? Are you okay?"

"I'm fine," she said with a sheepish smile. "Him? Not so much."

"What happened?"

"He tried to steal my purse, but I wasn't having it."

His gaze darted from the crook to Haley and back again. "What did you do?"

As they strolled toward the Land Rover, which was parked at the curb, Haley told Ashton what happened, and although she made light of the incident she was still shaken up. "It was the longest minute of my life," she confessed.

"Baby, I'm so proud of you. Standing up to that creep took a lot of guts, and few people could have done what you did."

His words touched her deeply.

"I better take you back to the hotel before you single-handedly wipe out all of the criminals in Caracas, and end up on every news station in the country!"

His joke lightened the mood, and laughing with Ashton helped ease her stress.

"I told you I was tough," she quipped despite her sweaty palms and shaking limbs. "I'm petite, but I can go toe-to-toe with anyone."

"But I don't want you to. Protecting you is my job, not yours."

"Ashton, I can take care of myself."

His tone was filled with concern. "You're my girl, and I don't want you in harm's way. That's why I suggested we go sightseeing together to reduce the risk of someone bothering you."

"No offense, but I wasn't raised in a gated mansion on a private island surrounded by nannies and butlers. I grew up in the inner city, and my parents taught me that common sense and discretion are essential to staying safe, so

I don't let anything stop me from living life to the fullest. The sooner you understand that the better off we'll be."

As they reached the SUV, Juan and Reynaldo jumped out of the Land Rover, but Ashton spoke to them in Spanish and they got back inside the car. Opening the trunk, he tossed the bags inside and pulled Haley into his arms.

"I'm just glad you're safe. You're important to me, Haley, and I don't know what I'd do if something bad ever happened to you."

Ashton held her close, and all was right with the world again. Closing her eyes, she reveled in the beauty of the moment. She'd never felt more loved or cared for, and his outpouring of affection aroused every inch of her body. Haley decided, right then and there, that tonight was the night. They were going to make love in her hotel suite, and it was going to be perfect. Remembering the slinky black negligee she'd bought hours earlier at the mall, Haley knew she'd chosen correctly. Ashton would take one look at her sexy outfit, sweep her up in his arms and head straight for the bedroom.

"Sir, I hate to interrupt," Reynaldo said, exiting the SUV for the second time in minutes. "But you're attracting attention, and I'm concered for your safety."

Reynaldo gestured across the street, and Haley noticed a group of men watching them.

"Thank you, Reynaldo."

Ashton opened the passenger side door. "Let's go, Rambo."

Tossing her head back, Haley burst out laughing. "Rambo? Is that my new nickname?"

"Yeah, do you like it?"

"No," she quipped, shaking her head. "Foxy Cleopatra sounds better."

Ashton winked. "Then Foxy Cleopatra it is."

Chapter 11

Haley stared at her reflection in the bedroom mirror of her hotel suite, loved what she saw and fluffed the curls tumbling around her face. Puckering her lips, she applied a second coat of red lipstick, then a spritz of perfume. She'd selected a white BCBG dress with a sweetheart neckline for her date with Ashton. Her look was sexy, but sophisticated, and she liked how the short, designer dress hugged her body in all the right places.

Sliding gold bangles onto her wrist, Haley noticed a faint bruise on her right arm and touched it with her thumb. Did that *really* happen? Did some crook actually try to mug her today? Haley covered the mark with a dab of concealer, then washed her hands. On the drive back to the hotel, she'd replayed the attack in her mind, and although she'd felt like crying she'd conquered her emotions and chatted with Ashton about his afternoon at the business summit. His speech was a hit, and they were going to celebrate at dinner.

Hearing a knock on the door, Haley turned off the bathroom light and rushed down the hallway, anxious to see Ashton. Scented candles cast a soft glow around the room and a tantalizing aroma from the suite's kitchen, courtesy of room service, inundated the air. Outside, the wind howled, and rain beat against the windows, but the suite was warm and cozy and the samba song playing on the stereo system made Haley feel like dancing. It had been pouring since they'd returned to the hotel an hour earlier, and although Ashton told her the weather conditions would improve, Haley didn't want to go out on the town. She wanted to spend a quiet evening in her suite with Ashton, not dining at an upscale restaurant, with his bodyguard and personal driver nearby.

Haley opened the front door, saw Ashton standing in the hallway in a black tailored suit, crisp white dress shirt and leather shoes, and moaned inwardly. Worried her knees would give way, Haley leaned against the door to support her weight. *What is the matter with me?* she thought, her gaze sliding down his toned physique. *Why am I panting?* Haley had to remind herself to breathe, and when Ashton bent down and kissed her cheek, desire engulfed her body. He complimented her outfit, telling her how pretty she looked, but her head was spinning so fast Haley couldn't respond.

"Are you ready to go? Reynaldo and Juan are holding the elevator for us."

"I was hoping we could stay in tonight."

An amused expression warmed his face. "It's going to stop raining, don't worry."

"I have a surprise for you." Haley took his hand, closed the door with her hips, and led him inside the suite. "Look, I ordered room service. Dinner's on me."

"Haley, that was very kind of you, but I insist on paying you back."

"Why? I work, and I enjoy spoiling the people I care about."

Ashton retrieved his wallet from his suit jacket, took out several hundred dollar bills and put them on the desk. "I'm a Rollins, Haley, and appearance means everything."

"Geez, what a drag. Don't you ever break the rules?"

"No, never. Do you?"

Haley grinned. "Every chance I get!"

Laughing, they intertwined fingers.

"Are you sure you want to stay in?" Ashton asked, brushing a stray curl away from her face. "Le Gourmet has an exceptional menu, and the staff are affable and polite."

"I'm sure. I want to have a quiet evening with my boyfriend. Is that too much to ask?"

"Not at all."

Ashton took out his cell phone, dialed a number, then spoke in Spanish. Haley didn't understand what he was saying, but suspected he was telling his staff about the last-minute change of plans. Seconds later, he ended the call and joined her inside the kitchen.

"I gave the guys the rest of the night off," he said with a smile. "Now I'm all yours."

I love the sound of that, Haley thought, feeling a rush of excitement.

Sniffing the air, Ashton patted his stomach. "I smell *arepas*."

"*Arepas*? What's that?"

"It's a staple of the Venezuelan diet. Locals eat them several times a day. They're corn cakes filled with gourmet cheese, fish, chicken and vegetables," he explained, taking off his suit jacket and chucking it on the couch. "What else did you order from room service?"

"I don't know." Haley giggled. "I told the hotel chef I'd

never eaten Venezuelan food before, and he assured me the meal would be healthy and delicious. Hopefully, he's right."

Ashton suggested they eat in the living room, and Haley agreed. He turned off the music, flipped on the TV and put on a movie. But once they started eating, the action flick was quickly forgotten. The *arepas* were flavorful but spicy and after a couple of bites Haley's mouth was on fire so Ashton ate the rest of it. He polished it off in seconds, then devoured three more.

The main course was seasoned with herbs and sautéed vegetables and Haley enjoyed everything about the bean dish entree and creamed chicken. Their conversation was full of flirtation, jokes and laughter, but what Haley loved most was how affectionate Ashton was. Holding her hand, he tenderly stroked her skin and praised her for being strong, and brave. No one had ever spoken to her with such admiration, and his words warmed her heart.

"I still can't believe you took down a mugger."

"Neither can I. It's the craziest thing I've ever done, but I have no regrets."

"Next time, I bet he'll think twice about robbing a tourist." He grinned, his eyes brightening with amusement. "I told Reynaldo and Juan what happened at Plaza Caracas, and they asked if you could show them your self-defense moves!"

Once they finished eating, Haley cleared their dirty plates, put them on the tray in the kitchen for room service and brought in the chocolate cake. "Do you have room for dessert?"

"Of course! It's my favorite meal of the day."

Haley cut a piece, put it on a gold-rimmed plate and set it on the coffee table. "Enjoy!"

"You're not having any cake? Why not? You love chocolate."

"I know, but if I keep eating everything in sight I won't be able to fit into the designer gown I bought for the anniversary party, and I can't afford to buy another dress."

"Haley, what are you talking about? You're stunning." Ashton pulled her down onto his lap and kissed her shoulder. "And I love how smart and witty you are, too."

"Well, you're the only one," she quipped, as painful memories scrolled through her mind. "My independence was a bone of contention with my ex-boyfriend. He accused me of being selfish and said I didn't know my place as a woman. Whatever that means."

"Is that why your relationship ended? Because he was intimidated by your strength?"

Haley started to speak, realized badmouthing her ex would make her look petty and took a moment to gather her thoughts. "Federico was a good guy from a wonderful family, but we wanted different things out of life and after a year of dating we decided to move on."

Ashton picked up the remote, lowered the volume on the flat-screen TV and tightened his arms around her waist. "How did you guys meet? Were you serious?"

Haley told Ashton about meeting Federico and his brother at a Home Depot workshop two years earlier. Bonding over their love of sports, family and Southern food, they'd become fast friends, and within weeks of meeting they were dating exclusively. A hopeless romantic, ready to settle down and start a family, she'd overlooked his jealous, controlling ways, convincing herself he'd change. He hadn't. And when Federico decided to move to the nation's capital Haley knew the universe was sending her a sign, and had broken up with him. "He wanted me to quit my job and relocate with him to Washington, but I just couldn't do it."

"Thank God you didn't. If you had, The Aunt Penny

Foundation would have lost a valuable employee, and we never would have met."

They shared a smile, and his soft caress along her legs tickled her skin.

"Why does your mom think you suck at relationships? Are you afraid of commitment?" she asked, recalling the conversation they'd had that morning when they'd arrived at the hotel. "How long has it been since you had a serious girlfriend?"

Ashton spoke fondly of his parents, namely his mom, but dodged her questions about his past relationships. Haley wanted details, but decided not to push him. He was stroking her shoulders, and it was hard to concentrate when all she could think of was ripping off his clothes and having her way with him on the sofa.

"I've been enamored with you since the first time I saw you, and the last few weeks with you have been incredible," he confessed. "I didn't realize how empty my life was until we met, but now that you're my girl I feel like I have it all."

At the sound of his deep, husky voice, her temperature rose. A tingle zipped down her spine, and Haley shivered involuntarily.

"I know I come on strong sometimes, but I'm not trying to control you." Taking her hand, he raised it to his mouth and kissed it. "You're important to me, Haley, and I just want to protect you."

His words penetrated the shield around her heart, causing it to crumble into pieces. His piercing gaze and the vulnerability in his voice were her undoing. Pushing her to act. To do what she'd been fantasizing about for weeks. Kissing him, she curled her arms around his neck, caressing the back of his head, then his broad, muscled shoulders.

They kissed for so long, with such passion and intensity Haley couldn't catch her breath. Trapping her tongue between his teeth, he licked and sucked the tip, teasing it with his own, arousing her body. Like chocolate and red wine, Ashton was her weakness. He made her want to do naughty things, and when he whispered dirty words in her ears Haley deepened the kiss.

"I'm glad you talked me into canceling our dinner reservations," he said, nibbling on the corner of her lips. "Because there's nothing better than being here with you."

Haley licked the rim of his ear with her tongue. "I *thought* you'd see things my way."

Undoing the buttons on his dress shirt, she stroked his bare chest, playfully pinched and tweaked his nipples. Haley couldn't stop touching him, wanting his hands all over her body, too. Brimming with confidence, she stood up, took off her dress and tossed it to the carpet. When she sat back down on his lap, his hands palmed her breasts through her bra, massaged and caressed them, but his eyes never left her face.

Wanting him to explore her body, she guided his hands down her hips and along her thighs. His fingers delved between her legs, touching her through her panties, and goose bumps exploded across her skin. The thrill of his caress caused her to moan as pleasure flooded her body. Desperate for him, Haley unzipped his pants, slid a hand inside his boxer briefs and stroked his package. His erection was long and thick and she wanted it buried deep inside her. It was time to consummate their relationship, and Haley was so excited about making love to Ashton she felt as if she was going to burst.

"I love what you're doing with your hands," Ashton praised her. Haley straddled his lap, massaging his erection with her pelvis.

"We better stop before we cross the line."

She didn't stop moving when she spoke. "There is no line, baby. Anything goes."

A frown wrinkled his smooth brow. "What are you saying?"

"I want to make love with you." It was a bold statement, one Haley couldn't believe had come out of her mouth, but it was the truth, and if she'd learned anything from dating Ashton it was to always speak her mind. "Please don't reject me. I don't think my heart could take it."

Cupping her face in his hands, he kissed her forehead, the tip of her nose and her cheeks. "I would never reject you. I want you every second of every day, but I don't want you to do something you're going to regret in the morning."

"I won't. I know what I want, and, baby, it's you."

His gaze narrowed, and Haley feared he didn't share her feelings. It was a mistake. She shouldn't have invited him into her suite for dinner, or asked him to spend the night with her. Was he hung up on someone else? Was that why he was rejecting her advances?

"This is so embarrassing." Feeling stupid for making the first move, Haley tried to stand, but Ashton tightened his hold around her waist. "Ashton, let go of me."

"No. I want you to stay. This is great. *You're* great, and I love being here with you."

"Then what is it? Why don't you want to make love? Don't you find me desirable?"

"Of course I do. You have an A-plus body and an A-plus mind, but the sexiest thing about you is definitely your smile. Every time you flash those pearly whites at me I hyperventilate!"

Haley giggled. Ashton made her laugh, cared about her as a person and was always doing things to make her smile. He had it all—good looks, a great job and a kind, gentle nature—and being with him made her feel like a teenager again.

"I invited you on the trip, hoping we'd make love, but now I'm having second thoughts. Our first time should be at my estate, not on a couch in a Caracas hotel."

His words surprised and confused her. "Why? Says who?"

"Haley, baby, you're special to me, and I want our first time to be memorable."

"It's not the location that matters, it's the feelings and emotions in our hearts." Haley gave him a sweet, soft kiss on the lips. She hadn't been intimate since she'd broken up with her ex, and Haley wanted Ashton so bad it was all she could think about.

Intertwining fingers, they moved closer to each other until their heads were touching.

"Haley, are you sure? I don't mind waiting—"

"Well, I do, so quit stalling."

Ashton chuckled, and Haley hoped she'd finally convinced him to spend the night.

"First one to the bedroom gets a massage!" she said, jumping to her feet.

"You're on!"

Giggling, Haley ran through the living room, with Ashton hot on her heels.

Chapter 12

Thunder boomed, lightning crackled, illuminating the somber gray sky, but Haley was in such a good mood nothing could dampen her spirits. Ashton brought out the best in her and she cherished every moment they spent together.

"Where do you think *you're* going?"

Ashton grabbed Haley from behind, tossed her onto the king-sized bed and jumped on top of her. She tried to escape, but he was too fast for her, and pinned her hands above her head. Ashton kissed her everywhere—her earlobes, along her neck and collarbone, and her erect nipples. His fingers slid across her stomach, tickling her, and she laughed out loud.

They took turns undressing each other, and as the rest of their clothes fell to the floor Haley realized there was no turning back. This was it. The moment she'd been waiting for. She'd wanted Ashton from the moment he'd walked into her office weeks ago, and she wasn't letting him out of her sight until she'd had her fill of him. If that was even possible. The more they kissed and caressed each other, the more she wanted to make love to him, and the ravenous expression on his face proved the feeling was mutual.

"You have a gorgeous body," she praised, caressing his chest.

A boyish smile covered his face. "I do?"

"Yes, Mr. Rollins, you do, and I'm looking forward to having my way with you tonight." To prove it, Haley rolled onto her side, opened the side drawer and took out the box of condoms she'd bought earlier at the mall. "May I?"

Nodding, Ashton wet his lips with his tongue. "Please do."

Haley took his erection in her hands. As she stroked it, images of fevered lovemaking bombarded her thoughts. Anxious for the main event, she rolled the condom onto his shaft and climbed on top of him. She'd never taken charge in the bedroom, but being in control with Ashton was a powerful, mind-blowing feeling. Haley guided his erection between her legs and slid it back and forth against her wetness.

Her skin tingled, and her heart beat raced. He wasn't even inside her yet, but she was already losing it. Grunting. Moaning. Licking and sucking his earlobes. Bucking wildly against him. Haley tried to stop the trembling in her legs, but an orgasm swirled through her body, and the shaking in her limbs intensified. Then Ashton thrust a finger inside her sex, and electricity shot through her core, knocking her flat on her back.

He kissed from her breasts to her feet, sending shivers down her spine. Sucking a toe into his open mouth, he licked it as if it was covered in chocolate, and Haley shrieked with laughter. It had never been like this before. Passionate. Freaky. So damn hot she feared she'd combust.

Ashton played in her curls, then slid a finger inside her

wetness. Then, nestling between her legs, he parted her lips with his tongue, and flicked it against her sex. One stroke, and pleasure coursed through her body. No one had ever volunteered to give her oral sex before, let alone enjoyed doing it, and seeing the proud expression on his face made her desire him even more.

Seconds passed, then minutes, and the longer Ashton sucked and licked her sex the harder it was for Haley to control herself. To stay in the moment. She felt out of it, delirious, and she couldn't stop grinding her sex against his face. Hiking her legs up, he nibbled and kissed her inner thigh. He took his time pleasing her, caressing her, and Haley loved every minute of it.

Closing her eyes, she buried her fingers in his hair, drawing his tongue deeper inside her sex. Moans streamed from her lips, bouncing off the ceilings and walls. It was heaven on earth. Ecstasy. The most thrilling moment of her life, and Haley didn't want it to ever end.

"I love how you feel, how you taste, how you smell," he said against her.

Love? Excitement danced inside her. Haley loved hearing the word come out of Ashton's mouth. Her heart was doing cartwheels inside her chest, but she wore a blank expression on her face. She didn't react. It was nothing, she told herself. A slip of the tongue. Just a figure of speech. No reason to get flustered and giddy. But as he whispered the words, butterflies swarmed her stomach. Haley wanted Ashton more than she'd ever wanted anyone, and his kisses were so thrilling and passionate she knew he'd be an exceptional lover between the sheets.

Ashton, I've fallen hard for you, she thought, overcome by the depths of her feelings. *You're unlike anyone I've ever met, and I love spending time with you. Please don't hurt me. I don't think I'd survive if you did.*

Memories of her ex-boyfriend barged into her thoughts, but Haley pressed her eyes shut, refusing to let her mind go there. She was with Ashton, and she didn't want to ruin the mood by thinking about her past. Tingling from her earlobe to her toes, Haley took a deep breath to regain control. It was too late. An orgasm sent shock waves through her core, and for the second time in minutes she collapsed onto the bed, gasping for air.

"Your beauty blows my mind," he said, coming up to her and brushing the tip of his nose against hers. "You're the total package, Haley. The one and only girl for me."

Haley smirked. "You're just saying that to get some ass."

"No way," he argued, adamantly shaking his head. "*You* seduced *me*, remember?"

"Is that what happened?" she asked feigning innocence.

They shared a smile, and Haley draped her arms around his neck, pulling him close.

"Baby, I want to settle down with you," he confessed. "You're it for me."

His smooth voice tickled her ears, and his tongue followed suit.

"You're the only woman I see in my future, the only woman I want."

Haley was simply overcome with emotion as his words played in her ears like a seventies love song.

"Then prove it," she challenged. "Show me what's in your heart."

"With pleasure."

Desperate for him, Haley pulled Ashton on top of her and clamped her thighs around his waist. One powerful thrust, and he was inside her. Moving slowly, caressing her, loving her. Making love to Ashton was everything she'd dreamed it would be, and for as long as Haley lived she'd never forget their first time. It was more than just sex. She felt connected to him, mind, body and soul, and knew no one would ever be able to take his place.

I love you, she thought, but wasn't brave enough to say. *I can take down a mugger twice my size, but I can't tell Ashton how I feel about him. What's up with that?*

Haley parted her lips, but fear held her captive. She'd never had a successful relationship, and was scared of getting hurt. But Haley was all for hooking up with Ashton, and she couldn't think of a more romantic venue for their first time than her posh hotel suite in Venezuela.

Ashton pressed his lips to her ear, then the curve of her neck, making circles with his tongue. His touch was addictive, his kiss breathtaking, his stroke the best thing that had ever happened to her body. Ashton was everything she'd ever wanted in a lover, and making love to him was everything she'd hoped it would be.

Haley clutched the silk sheets in her hands. Embarrassed that she was quivering beneath him, she clamped her lips together to stop from crying out. Never before had Haley experienced such pleasure and she was so overcome with emotion tears welled up in her eyes.

"Baby, tell me what you want, what you need. I want to please you."

"Ashton, you already have," she whispered against his mouth, staring deep into his eyes. "Being with you is like a dream. Every time we're together you make me feel like Cinderella, and this trip to Venezuela is the icing on the cake. What more could a girl want?"

His erection swelled inside her sex, filling her whole. Haley couldn't move. She was too weak, yet so blissfully happy. She cradled the back of his head in her hands and stroked his short brown hair.

Ashton did all the work. He moved faster, pumping harder, deeper, thrusting his hips like a male stripper under bright lights. He was breathing deeply, but he didn't stop. Only when she came apart beneath him did she feel his release. His body tensed, then he collapsed on the bed beside her, wearing a smile.

"You're going to be the death of me," he teased, giving her a peck on the lips. "You look all prim and proper in your tweed cardigans and sensible shoes, but you're a very bad girl in bed."

Sweat drenched her skin, but Haley snuggled against him. In a playful mood, he surprised her by cracking jokes, and even telling her stories about his childhood. Her body yearned for sleep, and when he kissed her softly on the lips and whispered, "Good night," Haley realized accompanying Ashton to Venezuela was the best decision she'd ever made. The COO was the real deal, the best boyfriend she'd ever had, and when Haley woke up from her nap she was going to put the rest of the chocolate cake—and her tongue—to good use.

Chapter 13

The eight-seat, motorized canoe pitched violently to the right, rocking back and forth in the Churún River, and Haley gripped Ashton's forearm so tight the veins in her hands throbbed. Water splashed into the boat, drenching her clothes, and she wiped her face with the sleeve of her fitted, white top. The sky was overcast, threatening rain, but Haley was sweating profusely.

"Before the 1930s, Angel Falls was an unknown wonder," announced the female tour guide. "American aviator James Crawford 'Jimmie' Angel discovered the falls while searching for gold, and after his death his family donated his Flamingo monoplane to the Aeronautics Museum of Maracay."

Haley blew out a deep, shaky breath. Her stomach was in knots. The lush, green scenery was amazing, and she was thrilled about their trip to Angel Falls, but she hated being in the small, wooden canoe. The tour guide kept the group engaged by sharing interesting facts about the popular tourist attraction, but Haley couldn't concentrate. Not when she was feeling queasy. It felt as if her life vest was choking her, and she feared if they didn't reach land soon she was going to get sick.

"Angel Falls is three times as tall as the Eiffel Tower in Paris, France," the tour guide droned.

Gazing at the sky, Haley tried to channel positive thoughts. It didn't work. If anything, it made her more nervous.

"At over eight hundred meters, Angel Falls is the highest waterfall in the world," the tour guide continued, her bright baby blues glued to Ashton. "It's fifteen times higher than Niagara Falls, and people travel far and wide to experience the mystical, magical waterfall."

Glad she'd had the foresight to put anti-nausea medication in her backpack that morning, Haley popped another pill into her mouth and washed it down with ginger ale.

The journey had been exhausting but Ashton assured her Angel Falls was worth it. The falls were located in an isolated jungle only accessible by boat. Once they reached the base of the mountain they'd hike to the falls. *Bring it on*, Haley thought, finishing her second bottle of ginger ale. *The sooner I get out of this boat the better.*

"This place is incredible," Ashton said, snapping pictures of the scenery with his high-tech camera. "I feel at peace, and one with nature. Don't you?"

Haley parted her lips, remembered the conversation they'd had last night in bed about the tour, and nodded in agreement instead of complaining about the choppy boat ride. Ashton had suggested renting a helicopter to take them to Angel Falls, but when Haley discovered the staggering cost, she'd talked him out of it. Just because Ashton was worth millions of dollars didn't mean she was comfortable with him spending money frivolously. But since she'd persuaded him to do the boat ride Haley knew she couldn't complain. He'd put a lot of effort into planning their trip and she didn't want to ruin his good mood. She'd never seen him so excited, and when he leaned over and kissed her cheek, happiness flooded her heart. Ashton made her feel safe and secure, and it was a remarkable feeling.

Her thoughts traveled to their romantic breakfast they'd enjoyed on her balcony that morning. Ashton had made her laugh until tears streamed down her cheeks, and remembering their playful, lighthearted banter brought a smile to her lips.

"I wish we could stay in Venezuela a few more days, but I have to fly back to Miami to oversee an important field test in the morning," he'd explained, forking a piece of turkey bacon into his mouth. "My dad isn't available, so I have to be there. Add to that, my schedule is swamped this week, and I want to get a head start on my monthly reports."

"I understand. I have meetings to prep for, several business dinners with important donors this week, and I'm volunteering at the soup kitchen as well, so I'm going to be crazy busy, too."

"Don't make plans for Saturday. We're having brunch with my parents at their estate."

"Baby, I wish you'd told me about it sooner. I can't go. I already have plans."

"With who, R.J. Johnson?" he'd asked, dropping his utensils on his plate.

His question confused her. "No, of course not. Why would you ask me that?"

"You left your email open on your laptop, and I saw the messages he sent you yesterday." His face had hardened like stone. "Tell him you have a boyfriend, or I will."

"Ashton, calm down. I'm not seeing R.J. on Saturday. I'm bringing Aunt Penny groceries, and we're going to spend the afternoon together. Hardly anything exciting."

Sighing in relief, he'd taken her hand and kissed it. "I'd love to meet your aunt."

For the second time in minutes, Haley's eyes had widened.

"We've been dating for several weeks now, and I've heard so much about Aunt Penny I feel like I already know her, so it would be great to finally put a face to the name."

It was the last thing she'd expected Ashton to say, and Haley was convinced she'd misheard him. "*You* want to meet my family?"

"It's only fair. You met my parents and passed with flying colors," he'd joked, with an amused expression on his face. "Now it's my turn to shine."

"You don't think it's too soon?"

"No. I've seen your birthmark. And I've sucked whip cream off your toes!"

And she'd loved every second of it, she'd thought, returning his smile. Aroused by the memory, her nipples had hardened and her legs had quivered under her purple silk robe.

"Haley, I'm proud to be your man, and I'd be honored to meet your family."

"Okay. Let's do it. We'll visit Aunt Penny on Saturday afternoon."

"Cool. After our visit you're coming to my place so pack an overnight bag."

"There you go giving out orders again," she'd quipped, rolling her eyes skyward. "I think you missed your calling. You should be an army sergeant, not a COO!"

"My bad." He'd flashed an apologetic smile. "Would you like to spend the night?"

"I can't. I'm having a slumber party for Sienna and her friends on Saturday night, and I have to be home to supervise them."

Ashton had cocked an eyebrow. “I love sleepovers. Can I come?” Dark and piercing, his eyes conveyed his feelings, and when he squeezed her hand and winked, Haley knew he was thinking about their tryst in the shower hours earlier. Haley enjoyed discovering what he liked, what turned him on, and took great pleasure in pleasing him.

“Nope. The back-to-school slumber party is for the girls in the Aunt Penny mentorship program, not for bad boys who like to get their freak on.”

“You’re a fine one to talk,” he’d shot back, barking a laugh. “You covered my body with chocolate icing last night while I was sleeping, and hungrily licked it off!”

Handsome in his striped shirt and khaki shorts, he’d charmed her with his boyish smile, and they’d spent hours on the balcony flirting and laughing. “I can’t see you this weekend, but I’m free next Saturday. Would that work? We’ll visit Aunt Penny on the fifteenth, then spend the rest of the weekend together at your estate.”

“Sounds good to me.”

“Then it’s a date.”

“Don’t make plans for the twenty-first,” Ashton said. “My parents are dragging me to the symphony and I want you to be my date.”

“I’d love to. Before Aunt Penny got sick, we used to go see shows regularly.”

His cell had buzzed, drawing his gaze to the table, and he’d picked it up.

“Don’t even *think* of answering your phone,” she’d quipped, pointing her butter knife at his plate. “We’re still eating, and we’re not finished discussing the Angel Falls tour.”

“When did you get so bossy?”

A smile had tugged at her lips. “When you had your way with me in the shower.”

"I had my way with you? No, babe, it was the other way around."

"You enjoyed every minute of it." Standing, she'd untied the belt on her robe and straddled his lap. "So, you want to have a quickie, right here, right now. Right?"

"Damn," he'd growled, cupping her ass in his hands. "You know me so well."

Haley didn't realize the canoe had stopped until Ashton clasped her hand and helped her to her feet. After an exhausting boat trip they'd finally reached the base of the falls, and Haley was so relieved she did the Happy Dance along the river bank. Everyone laughed, and once Ashton took their backpacks out of the boat they set off for the hike.

Multicolored birds flew in the sky, insects chirped, and the air held the scent of rain. The falls were buried deep in the, Canaima National Park, which was filled with tropical plants, leafy flowers and exotic wildlife. A thick haze drifted over the horizon, but it didn't detract from the beauty of their surroundings. An indigenous man in a feathered headpiece and a brown tunic passed them on the steep, narrow trail, and Haley felt as if she'd stepped back in time.

The trail was slippery and wet, and even though Haley was tired she kept up with Ashton and their travel companions. Bothered by the heat, she took off her floppy hat and stuffed it into her backpack. Stripping down to her bikini top, she wet her hands and shorts-clad legs in the water to cool down, then drank the rest of her ginger ale.

The sky cleared, the sun emerged from the clouds and a humid breeze ruffled the tree branches. By the time they reached the peak of Angel Falls, Haley was bubbling with enthusiasm and excitement. Gawking at the view, she marveled at the world around her. The jagged rock formations, the cascading waters, the Crayola-green trees and serene, picture-postcard views.

Walking up from behind, Ashton enveloped her in his arms and kissed her shoulder. "I've been here before, but it's more beautiful than I remember."

"Baby, you were right," she said, stroking his forearms. "Angel Falls was definitely worth the trip, and I wouldn't want to be here with anyone but you."

"Not even R.J. 'Seduce-'em-and-bed-'em' Johnson?"

"Oh, stop. That man doesn't stand a chance with me."

His eyes brightened with interest. "He doesn't?"

"Boy, please, not even if he begged." Haley tenderly caressed his cheek, then softly kissed his lips. "My boyfriend does yoga, and he's so flexible he can do all of the positions in the Kama Sutra—even the impossible ones!"

Chuckling, their laugher bouncing off the mountain, they shared another kiss.

For hours, they snapped pictures, took videos on their cell phones and splashed in the coral-blue water cascading off the falls. Haley was starving, but Ashton was having so much fun playing kickball with Reynaldo and Juan she didn't want to interrupt him for lunch. Watching them run around and goof off made her laugh. They were flying back to Miami that evening, but Haley wished they could spend another week in Venezuela. There was so much to see and do in the country, and she wanted to learn more about the culture.

Their eyes met, and Ashton must have read her thoughts because he grabbed his Nike backpack. He spoke to Reynaldo quietly for several seconds, waved goodbye to the two men, then headed straight for her, wearing a broad smile.

"Ready to eat? I know the perfect spot."

Confused, Haley frowned. "Is there somewhere around here to buy food?"

"No." Adjusting his Firebirds baseball cap, he gestured

to his backpack. “Everything we need is in here. Come on, baby. Let’s go. I’m starving.”

Clasping her hand, Ashton led her carefully down the mountain. In a jovial mood, he shared interesting facts about Angel Falls and Canaima National Park as they trekked through the jungle. Haley enjoyed listening to him, and cracked up when Ashton joked about his vacation-from-hell to Venezuela with his parents a decade earlier.

Haley could hear the distant sound of splashing water, people speaking Spanish and knew they were near the base of the falls. Surprised, she glanced at her watch. She’d been having so much fun with Ashton, talking and laughing about their families and friends, she’d lost track of time and was shocked to see it was already two o’clock. They’d been at Angel Falls for three hours, but Haley didn’t want to leave. She was having a blast with Ashton, and wanted to create more wonderful memories with him.

“It was the worst vacation I’ve ever had, and even though it’s been many years since I traveled to Merida with my parents, I still have nightmares about that gondola ride!”

“I’m an only child, too, so I feel your pain,” Haley said. “I’ll be twenty-nine in December, but my parents still treat me like a kid, and it can be frustrating.”

“At least you don’t work with your dad. I do, and it’s incredibly stressful.”

“Have you always dreamed of working in the family business?”

“When I was five, my grandfather George gave me a vintage airplane, and that sparked my interest in aviation. After a trip to the Museum of Flight in Seattle a couple years later, I became obsessed with planes, and the rest is history.”

Ashton stopped near a thicket of trees off the paved trail, and spread a blue wool blanket on the ground. Opening his backpack, he unloaded several food containers. Eyes wide, Haley couldn't believe he had quesadillas, tropical fruit, ice-cold drinks and even pastries.

"Where did you get all this food?" Haley asked, scratching her head.

"At the Canaima Village. I purchased everything in the market while you were in the ladies' room, and Reynaldo offered to carry the bag since my hands were already full."

As they ate, they looked at the pictures and videos he'd taken at the falls with his camera, and discussed their favorite parts of the trip. Haley ate two plates of food, but when Ashton pressured her to have dessert she tossed her napkin at him.

"You're bad for me," she joked, tearing her gaze away from the container of hazelnut brownies. "You take me to fancy restaurants and feed me exotic foods constantly. How am I supposed to stay slim and trim when you're always tempting me with chocolate?"

"Are we still talking about food, or the *other* dessert you like?"

"Ashton, I'm serious. I'm gaining weight by the second."

"I never noticed."

"Then you're blind, because I've put on ten pounds since we met," she confessed. "At this rate I'll never fit into the dress I bought for the Millionaire Moguls anniversary party at the end of the month."

Ashton shrugged. "Don't sweat it. I'll buy you another one. And anything else you need. Baby, I got you. You know that."

He made her feel more desirable than Miss Universe, and his sensuous French kiss caused her pulse to race and her heart to dance. It had been a perfect day, one she'd remember for as long as she lived, and being with Ashton made Haley rethink her punishing work schedule. For years, she'd worked ten-hour days, six days a week, but not anymore. Why slave away at her desk when she could spend time with a caring, compassionate man who treated her like a queen? The kiss intensified, and Haley slipped a hand under his shirt, stroking his chest.

"Are Juan and Reynaldo meeting us here?"

"No. They'll call me when the boat arrives. Why?"

"I just wanted to make sure we're alone," she explained, nibbling on his bottom lip. Having sex in public had always been her fantasy, and Haley wanted to make her dreams come true. "I hate being interrupted when I'm seducing my man."

"Is that what this is? A game of seduction?"

"Absolutely. Why let this incredible scenery go to waste?"

"Someone might see us."

"Then you better make this quick!"

Chuckling, he slid his gaze down the length of her body. "I love how you think," Ashton whispered against her ear. "And I love how sexy your ass looks in these teeny-tiny denim shorts. You're so hot I can't get enough of you."

Wanting privacy, Haley pulled the blanket over them and pressed her body flat against his. His kiss made her yearn for more, arousing her all over. He unbuttoned her shorts and yanked them down her hips. Rubbing his erection against her sex, Ashton made her horny, and wet. His fingers dove between her legs, swirling, caressing and playing in her curls, and she thrust her hips upward, eager for more.

Knowing they didn't have much time, she took his erection out of his shorts and eagerly stroked it with her hands. It hardened, doubling in size, and her eyes widened at the sight of his incredible length. Her mouth watered, and a shudder zipped through her body.

"Put it in your mouth," he instructed. "Suck me until I'm good and hard."

"With pleasure." Climbing on top of him, her head facing his groin, Haley parted her lips and swirled her tongue around his erection.

"Reverse cowgirl. My favorite position. How did you know?"

Smiling, Haley nipped at the tip of his shaft with her teeth. "Lucky guess."

He kissed her ass, squeezing and massaging it with his hands, and Haley moaned out loud. Panting, she responded enthusiastically to his touch, shamelessly begging him for more.

Heat flooded her skin, and tingles shot down her spine. Overcome with desire, Haley tossed her head back as contractions rocked her body.

Ashton pulled Haley to his chest, rolled onto his side, and entered her in one, swift motion. Welcoming him inside, she pressed her butt against his groin, and hooked an arm around his leg. He thrust his erection deep inside her, stealing her breath, filling every inch of her. From behind, Ashton cupped her breasts, tugging and tweaking her erect nipples, and Haley cried out.

Their lovemaking was passionate and intense, so thrilling and exciting she thought she was dreaming. But his touch was real. The warmth and pleasure of his kiss made goose bumps prickle her skin. Haley was in the forest, making love to Ashton, and it was incredible.

Glancing over her shoulder, she watched his erection move in and out of her sex. Turned on, a groan fell from her lips. Haley pulled his face toward her, and kissed him, teasing his tongue with her own. Ashton gave her exactly what she needed, what her body was craving. Did all the things she'd begged him for last night in her hotel suite. Pulled her hair, tickled her earlobe with his tongue, spanked and squeezed her ass. They were one, connected mind, body and soul, and Haley had never felt more alive.

Clenching the muscles between her legs intensified the depth and penetration of his stroke, and when Ashton cursed in Spanish, Haley knew the spine-tingling sensation had coursed through his body, too. Her moans and shrieks inundated the air, echoing off the mountains.

"Baby, keep it down," Ashton whispered against her mouth. "Someone will hear you and alert the park rangers, and I don't want to get arrested in Venezuela for public indecency."

His words went in one ear and out the other. Haley couldn't stop. Couldn't control herself. She'd lost that ability the moment he'd plunged his erection inside her, and the faster he pumped his hips the louder she groaned his name. An orgasm claimed her body, and stars and lights exploded in her eyes.

Increasing his pace, Ashton clutched her hips. As he climaxed, he threw his head back, and the sound of his heavy breathing filled the air. Haley stroked his neck and his shoulders, nibbled playfully on his chin. For several seconds, he remained perfectly still, then collapsed onto the blanket, where he gathered her in his arms and kissed her softly on the lips.

Hot under the blanket, Haley tossed it aside and rested her head on his chest. His heart was racing, beating out of control, and sweat glistened on his creamy brown skin. The air smelled of flowers, and the fragrant aroma made Haley yearn for a bubble bath and a glass of red wine. "You're amazing, you know that?" she said, caressing his face.

"You're an extraordinary woman, Haley, and I love being with you."

"Baby, that's so sweet. No one's ever called me extraordinary before."

"I'm glad I'm the first." Playing in her hair, he gazed deep into her eyes. "I felt an immediate connection to you, and I knew one day we'd be lovers."

Her heart stopped. "Is that all we are? Secret lovers?"

"Of course not. Isn't it obvious how I feel about you? How much I desire you?"

He sounded hurt, and Haley felt bad for bruising his feelings.

"After I lost my fiancée, I never thought I'd find love again."

"You were engaged? When? For how long? What happened?"

"It was a long time ago." A pained expression crossed his face, but he cupped her chin in his hand and showered her mouth in soft, tender kisses. "Haley, I don't want you for just one night. I want you every night, for the rest of my life."

Her lips parted wordlessly. Haley was glad she was lying down, because if she'd been standing her knees would have buckled, and she would have fallen to the ground.

"You're everything I want in a woman, and I have every intention of making you my wife," he confessed. "I want you to be Mrs. Ashton Rollins one day."

Seeing his eyes light up, Haley smiled. She wanted to tell Ashton how much she loved him, but her confidence deserted her when he tossed aside the blanket and took his cell phone out of his back pocket. "Baby, we have to go."

"Why?" she asked, flashing a cheeky smile. "We're not finished *exploring*."

Grinning, Ashton slowly shook his head. "You're insatiable, you know that?"

"I can't help it. You're an incredible lover, and I enjoy making love to you."

"Baby, we can't."

"Of course we can," she purred, licking his earlobe. "I'll be quick. I promise."

Ashton held up his cell phone. "Reynaldo just texted me. The boat is here, and if we miss it we won't make our eight o'clock flight, and I have to return to Miami tonight."

To make him laugh, Haley rolled her eyes and stuck out her tongue. "Party pooper!"

They got dressed, tossed everything into Ashton's backpack and jogged down the trail in search of Reynaldo and Juan. Finding them at the base of the falls, they walked along the shore and got inside the canoe. As they headed back down the river, chatting and laughing about their day, it dawned on Haley that Ashton had never answered her questions about his ex-fiancée. Why wouldn't he open up to her about his ex? He was honest about everything except his past relationships, and Haley wanted to know what he was hiding.

Haley glanced at Ashton, noticed the pensive expression on his face and wondered if he was thinking about his fiancée. It was a troubling thought. Questions plagued her mind, intensifying her fears and doubts. Was he carrying a torch for his ex? Did he want her back? "Ashton, can I ask you something—"

He crushed his lips to her mouth, kissing her with such passion Haley lost her train of thought. His hands felt warm against her cheek, and her body responded eagerly to his touch. Haley wanted to slide onto Ashton's lap and pick up where they'd left off in the woods, but getting frisky with him in the canoe was a bad idea. Once they started making out, there was just no stopping them, so she ended the kiss and dropped her hands to her sides. Out of the corner of her eye, she noticed the tour guide watching them. *That's right*, Haley thought, snuggling against his chest. *He's mine. All mine!*

"I want to see you tomorrow night." His tone was silky smooth "I'm taking you for sushi, so don't make any other plans. I'll pick you up at work at six o'clock, so be ready to go when I get there."

"It's a date. Should I bring my overnight bag?"

His eyes twinkled with mischief, and Haley knew what Ashton was going to say before the words left his mouth. "Hell yeah, and don't forget the whipped cream."

Chapter 14

"Honey, where are you?" As she marched through the foyer of Ashton's estate, Joan's high-heel shoes smacked against the marble floors, and her loud, strident voice echoed off the alabaster walls. "I saw your Mercedes parked in the driveway, and the hood is still warm, so don't bother trying to hide from me. I *know* you're here, and I'm not going anywhere until we talk."

Outside on the deck, putting spare ribs on the grill to slow-cook, Ashton listened to his mother rant and rave about how selfish and inconsiderate he was. Passionate and animated, with a flair for the dramatic, Joan should have been an actress instead of a trophy wife. Whenever Ashton teased her about being his "movie star," she'd giggle.

"Mom, I'm on the deck," he called, slathering barbecue sauce all over the ribs. "Grab a bottle of wine and join me outside."

Appearing at the French doors, she crossed her arms and stared him down. Ashton took one look at his mom and knew he was in trouble. Why was she glaring at him? What had he done now? He racked his brain for answers, but came up empty. He couldn't fathom what he'd done to upset her, but he wanted to make amends.

Ashton lowered the volume on the stereo system with the remote control, and nodded in greeting. "Hi, Mom, it's great to see you. What brings you by?"

"Don't even try it," she snapped, walked up to him and jabbed an index finger at his chest. "I'm very upset with you, young man, and that boyish smile isn't going to save you this time."

Confused, he stared blankly. Worry lines wrinkled Joan's forehead, her lips were pursed, and her posture was so stiff she looked like a mannequin in a store window.

"How can you be so insensitive?"

Squinting, Ashton shielded his eyes from the sun. The sky was still bright, blazing with sunshine, and the air was hot and humid. It was the perfect weather for a barbecue, or for frolicking in the pool, and Ashton liked the idea of splashing around with Haley in the water. First he'd feed her, then he'd make love to her.

Turned on by the thought, he remembered his conversation with Haley that morning. Missing her, he'd phoned her from his Mercedes as he was driving to work and invited her over for dinner. When she'd hesitated, Ashton had poured on the charm. It worked every time. Not that he was playing games. Other guys were interested in her too—wealthy, successful businessmen like R.J. Johnson—and Ashton wanted Haley to know he was a hundred percent committed to her. To prove it, he'd made time to see her every day that week. On Monday he'd treated her to a delicious meal at a Japanese restaurant. On Tuesday he'd taken her to a comedy club, and yesterday they'd attended a free workshop at Home Depot. Ashton couldn't get enough of her, and he had been so anxious for Haley to arrive he'd kept sneaking glances at his Rolex watch. Every day, he found new things to admire about her, and he loved the idea of them living together as husband and wife.

Ashton didn't want to argue with his mom, but when she insulted him he spoke up.

"We haven't seen each other all week, so I don't understand why you're mad at me."

"*That's* the problem. I haven't heard from you since you returned from Venezuela."

Her voice was small, tinged with pain, and Ashton feared Joan would break down in tears. That would be a disaster. Haley would be at the estate in a couple hours, and he didn't want anything to ruin their date. He wanted to make her smile, and a home-cooked meal at his estate was sure to brighten her day. They'd talked at lunchtime, and she'd sounded so upset Ashton had considered driving to the foundation to see her. One of the students she mentored was having problems at home, and Haley was worried sick about the troubled teen.

"Mom, my schedule is insane right now. You know that."

"That's no excuse. Why haven't you called or dropped by for a visit? I miss you."

His heart softened. Seeing the wounded expression on Joan's face bothered him, so he made a mental note to take her out for dinner next week. Being an only child, he knew it was important to spend quality time with his mom, and he hoped taking Joan to her favorite restaurant would cheer her up. If it didn't, he'd buy her a diamond brooch from Cartier.

Ashton put down the bowl, wiped his hands on his checkered apron and kissed his mom on the cheek. "I'm sorry. I've been busy with work, getting everything in place for the Moguls anniversary party, and wining and dining my amazing new girlfriend, but I had every intention of coming by with Haley on Sunday—"

"Haley?" Her face brightened. "You're still dating her?"

"Absolutely. She's an incredible woman, and I adore her."

Joan clasped her hands together and did a twirl, causing her sleek, black hair to whip around her face. "Honey, that's wonderful! I was terrified you'd die alone in this big, beautiful house, so I'm thrilled that you've finally found someone special."

"You are?"

"God, yes. You haven't been serious with anyone since Mia passed away, and I'd lost all hope of ever having a daughter-in-law." Squealing, Joan wrapped her arms around his waist and squeezed so hard he thought he heard his ribs crack. "This is fantastic news! I'm so happy I could weep!"

Amused by his mother's reaction, Ashton returned her hug. He'd never see her this excited, and was glad he'd confided in her about Haley. He wondered if he should tell her the rest of what was on his mind.

It pissed him off that other men were romantically interested in his girlfriend, and although he kept a close eye on her when they were out together in public, he'd feel more secure if they were engaged. Though, he knew he'd have to open up to Haley about his past before he proposed.

Just the thought of telling her about Mia and the accident made his stomach churn. Ashton never talked about the car crash, but he couldn't risk Joshua or Becca telling Haley first.

His mom's delighted voice broke through his thoughts. "Any idea when I can expect my first grandchild?"

"One thing at a time, Mom," he said, laughing. "First we have to get engaged."

"Then pop the question tonight. No time like the present, right?"

Ashton met her gaze. She was serious! He wouldn't have been more surprised if his dad had burst into the kitchen, jumped onto the table and did the Macarena. "Mom, slow down! I'm not ready to propose just yet, but it has been on my mind a lot the last few weeks."

"Why wait? When it comes to matters of the heart you have to be aggressive. Women love that." Talking with her hands, Joan gestured to the French doors. "Let's go to Cartier. I'm free tonight, and you know there's nothing I love more than shopping for jewelry."

His mom could spend hours talking about his love life and her burning desire to have grandchildren, but Ashton didn't have time to shoot the breeze with Joan. He still had to shower and change.

"Mom, I can't. Haley will be here soon, and I want dinner to be ready by the time she arrives. She's coming straight from work, and she's probably starving."

Joan patted his cheek. "My son, the chef. Who would have thought?"

Certainly not him. He hated cooking, but he loved spoiling Haley. Smiling, he added the vegetables to the grill and lowered the temperature. "Where's Dad?"

"Doing what he does best."

"Work!" they said in unison, sharing a knowing smile.

His cell phone rang, and Ashton read the number on the screen. He didn't feel like talking to Joshua but took the call. "Hello, Joshua," he said calmly.

"I've been calling you for weeks with no luck. Didn't you get my messages?"

"I've been busy. What do you want?"

Joshua cleared his throat. "I need to speak to you in private. It's important."

"Now is not a good time. I'm visiting with my mom."

"I understand. Are you free tomorrow for lunch?"

He was, but he didn't want to break bread with Joshua DeLong, he thought, a scowl curling his lips. Ashton knew his schedule like the back of his hand, but he faked uncertainty. "Don't know for sure. I'll double-check my agenda, and have my secretary call you first thing in the morning."

"Excellent. I look forward to hearing from her."

Ashton hit the end button and placed his cell phone on the table. Joshua had some nerve calling him after everything he'd done. He was a snake who was trying to unseat him as president, but Ashton wasn't going down without a fight.

"Ashton, are you listening to me?"

Deep in thought about the power struggle within Prescott George, Ashton apparently hadn't heard anything his mother had been saying. He felt guilty that she'd caught him daydreaming. "Mom, of course I'm listening to you. You're my number one girl, and that will never change."

Her smile returned. Taking a seat at the table, Joan patted the chair beside her, and Ashton reluctantly sat down. Opening one of the glass bowls, she helped herself to a garlic cheese roll and popped it into her mouth.

"I want to invite Haley to my Women of Distinction Tea next Friday," she explained, dabbing her lips with a napkin. "There will be a lot of generous, charity-minded women at the estate, and I want them to meet my future daughter-in-law."

Ashton swallowed a laugh. Joan talked a good game, but he was no fool. His mom and her rich, uppity friends wanted to grill Haley about her family, her educational background, her dating history and her ten-year-goals, but Ashton wasn't having it.

"Mom, that's very sweet of you, but we volunteer at the Miami Soup Kitchen on Friday nights, and if Haley's not there to make her delicious seafood gumbo the regulars will complain."

Joan raised a thin, perfectly plucked eyebrow. "*You* volunteer at the Miami Soup Kitchen?" she asked, her tone thick with disbelief. "Since when?"

"Since Haley invited me. I've volunteered a few times, and I really enjoyed it. So much so, I look forward to going every week," he confessed.

Her eyes popped. "You do?"

Ashton nodded. "I didn't realize how sheltered I was until I met Haley, but she's showed me a whole new world, and her positive influence has changed me for the better."

"I wouldn't be caught dead at the Miami Soup Kitchen." Like a ghost, Alexander appeared in the outdoor living room, a cigar dangling from between his pursed lips. "It's frequented by crooks and bums, and I don't want to get robbed."

Put off by his self-righteous attitude, Ashton said, "Good thing I'm me and not you."

Father and son locked eyes, and the stench of their animosity polluted the night air.

Chapter 15

A shiver snaked down Ashton's spine, but he returned his father's cold, dark stare and didn't flinch when Alexander stepped forward. Noticing his dad's furrowed brows and clenched jaw, Ashton wondered what his problem was. Anything could set him off—traffic jams, bad weather, stray cats—and everyone in the Rollins family walked on eggshells whenever he was in a bad mood.

Ashton scrutinized Alexander's appearance. His dad lived in Armani suits and silk ties, so Ashton was surprised to see him dressed in a polo shirt, linen slacks and loafers. Then he remembered it was Thursday night, and his dad was going to the country club to play chess with his friends from Prescott George. "Dad, what's the matter?" Ashton opened the grill to check on the spare ribs, and the heady aroma made his mouth water. "As usual, you look pissed—"

"Don't talk to me like that. I'm your father, not one of your subordinates."

Then act like it, he thought, annoyed by his dad's curt tone.

Taking a seat at the table, Alexander puffed vigorously on his Cuban cigar. Smoke billowed in the air, and the odor made Ashton's stomach churn. Why did his dad insist on smoking when his mom hated it? Didn't he care about anyone besides himself? he wondered, waving a hand in front of his face. And why the hell was he smoking on *Ashton's* property?

"Great timing, dear. Our son has big news." Beaming, Joan fingered her pearl necklace. Dressed in a green safari jacket, loose-fitting blouse and cropped khaki pants, she looked chic and sophisticated. "Ashton's going to propose to Haley!"

His lips a hard line, Alexander fervently shook his head. "That's stupid. Only a moron would propose to a woman he's only known for a month."

No one asked you, so mind your business, old man, Ashton thought, struggling to keep his temper in check. Talking to his dad was emotionally and mentally draining, and he wanted him to leave. He had things to do, and arguing with his dad wasn't one of them.

With the help of Ms. Edith, he'd prepared all of Haley's favorites—chicken shish kebabs, cranberry pecan salad, grilled lobster, barbecue ribs—and couldn't wait for her to taste his cooking. Wanting to be alone with her, he'd given his staff the rest of the night off, but now he regretted his decision. He still had to set the table, light the candles and make dessert. Pressed for time, Ashton considered asking his mom for help, but thought better of it. If he did, she'd never leave, and he wanted his parents gone ASAP. "Dad, relax. I'm not proposing to Haley tomorrow, or even next month, but it's definitely something I'm thinking about."

"Date for a year," Alexander advised, his tone stern. "And if you're still gung-ho about getting married, your mother and I will give you our blessing."

Joan spoke up. "Too late. I already did. There's no reason for Ashton to wait. The sooner he settles down and gets married, the better."

Alexander scoffed. "Spoken like a hopeless romantic with absolutely no insight."

"I'm not getting any younger, and neither are you," she pointed out. "I want to be a young, hip grandma who can chase her grandkids around the park, not a doddering, old granny who can't keep up."

"He can't propose to that girl. I forbid it."

Ashton clenched his fists so hard his knuckles cracked. He loved his dad and wanted to make him proud, but he hated his pessimistic attitude. Besides, the older Alexander got, the more cantankerous he was, and it was getting harder and harder to be around him.

"He barely knows her," Alexander argued, puffing vigorously on his cigar. "What if she tricks him, steals his money, then publicly humiliates him? What then?"

Ashton knew it was a mistake to argue with his dad, but he had to speak his mind. "Haley's not like that. She's smart, and ambitious and independent, and she'd never do anything to hurt me. Everything in me is telling me that Haley's the one, and I'm not letting her go."

His mother nodded. "I feel the same way, son. She's a keeper, so don't screw this up. I want grandkids, and the more the better!" Dancing around in her chair, Joan helped herself to a chicken shish kebab from the glass dish and took a bite. "I love the idea of a winter wedding, Ashton. Don't you?"

His father scoffed. "What if I'm right and Haley turns out to be a gold digger with an agenda?"

"I'll survive." An image of Mia, prostrate in a white casket, flashed in his mind. Pain stabbed his heart. Swallowing hard, Ashton blinked away the tears that swam in his eyes. Petite and adorable, with a shy demeanor, Mia, had filled his life with happiness and joy, and for as long as he lived she'd always have a special place in his heart. "If I can survive losing my fiancée in a horrific car crash, I can overcome anything."

Ashton coughed into his fist, took a moment to gather himself. His cell phone rang, but he ignored it. He'd never spoken to his parents about the accident, or the grief he'd experienced for years, but Ashton wanted them to know they couldn't control him anymore. It was his life, and he wasn't going to let his father boss him around.

"Dad, I don't care what you think anymore. I decide what's best for me, not you—"

Feeling a hand on his forearm, Ashton broke off speaking and glanced at his mom.

In the past, whenever he'd argued with his dad, Joan would always intervene, but not this time. She sat beside him, shoulder to shoulder, nodding her head in agreement. Encouraged and thankful for her support, Ashton continued.

"From day one, you tried to break me and Mia up, but it didn't work back then, and it damn sure isn't going to work now. I'm going to continue dating Haley whether you like it or not, and there's nothing you can do about it."

"Mia was a nobody, and marrying her would have tarnished our family name."

Joan dropped her hand to her side. "Honey, your father's right," she said, with a sad smile. "I never wished the girl any harm, but I'd be lying if I said I liked her. I didn't."

"Neither did I," Alexander said. "Mia was using you, but you were too blind to see it."

Before Ashton could respond, his father spoke.

"Forget about that Haley girl and focus on confronting

Joshua DeLong," he ordered. "Or you'll be axed, and *he'll* be the new president of Prescott George."

Ashton opened his mouth to argue, realized he had no words and slammed it shut.

"Joshua has more support than you realize, and your approval rating is lower than ever. It's just a matter of time before you're out and Joshua is in."

Damn. His dad was right. He had to confront Joshua. Set him straight. Remind him who was in charge. He'd arrange a meeting with him after the anniversary party. And if the corporate raider double-crossed him, he'd make him pay. No one was unseating him as president. He loved the organization, and had given it his all for the past five years. Furthermore, his grandfather and father had been president of Prescott George for decades before him, and when Ashton was ready to step down as president, his future son or daughter—not a troublemaker like Joshua DeLong—would replace him.

"I won't let you ruin my reputation or the Rollins family legacy," Alexander raged, banging his fist on the table. "You better get your act together, *fast*, or you're going to destroy everything your grandfather and I worked so hard for."

Anger boiled in Ashton's veins, but he didn't lash back at his dad. There was no point. Besides, he had a date to get ready for.

But nothing stopped Alexander Rollins.

"Son, think!" Alexander tapped his temples with a finger. "You have to stay one step ahead of him. He's sly and crafty, and if you underestimate him he'll screw you over."

Fed up, Ashton pushed back his chair and jumped to his feet. Anxious to get away from his dad, he pocketed his cell and stalked through the outdoor living room. His dad was pissing him off, and he couldn't stand to be around him another second. Alexander talked so much a telemarketer would hang up on *him*, and Ashton was sick of his insults and negativity.

"Where do you think you're going?" Alexander said.

"To get ready for my date. Mom, Dad, please see your way out."

"Ashton, honey, wait! Come back!"

Joan sounded frantic, like a mother who'd lost her child in the shopping mall, but Ashton continued through the French doors and jogged upstairs. In the master bedroom, he kicked off his sandals, stripped down to his boxer briefs and grabbed a towel from his walk-in closet. Hearing his cell phone buzz, he picked it up and punched in his password.

Please call me back. It's important.

Reading Haley's text message, Ashton sensed something was wrong and dialed her immediately. She answered on the first ring, and hearing her voice instantly brightened his mood. His anger evaporated, and a smile warmed his lips. "Hey, babe, are you on your way?"

Ashton heard noises in the background, and suspected Haley was still at work. No surprise. Because of her responsibilities at the foundation, she was often late for their dates, but tonight Ashton didn't mind. He could use the extra time to prepare for their romantic dinner.

"Something's come up. I can't make it tonight."

The weight of his disappointment caused his knees to buckle and Ashton sank onto his king-sized bed. "What's going on? Is everything okay?"

"One of the students I mentor really needs me right now, and I want to be there for her."

"Is it Sienna?" he asked, recalling previous conversations about the teen.

"Yes." Lowering her voice, Haley spoke in a whisper. "Her mom's boyfriend tried to force himself on her last night, and Sienna's still pretty shaken up about it. Her friends brought her to the center about an hour ago, and she's napping on my office couch right now."

"Damn. What a creep. Want me and some of my friends to pay him a visit?"

"No, thanks. I can handle him."

Hearing the edge in her voice, Ashton tried to lighten the mood. "Oh, no," he joked. "Look out. Foxy Cleopatra strikes again!"

Haley giggled. "Thanks for the laugh, babe. I needed that. It's been a crummy day."

Mission accomplished, Ashton thought, his chest puffed up with pride. "I'm going to be up late, so if you change your mind, come by. I'd love to see you. I *need* to see you."

His confession, and the vulnerability in his voice, surprised him, but Ashton didn't regret speaking from the heart. Haley was a caring and loving girlfriend who supported him wholeheartedly, and her boundless enthusiasm was infectious. Born into a wealthy family, he'd never struggled for anything, but meeting Haley made him want to be a better man. He now felt compelled to give back to the community in a meaningful, tangible way, and he also wanted to invest in Miami's youth.

"It's been a long day for me, too," he said, "and I could use some of your positive energy right now."

"Sienna's staying at my place tonight, and I don't want to leave her alone," she said quietly. "You'll be at the soup kitchen tomorrow night, and we're still on for Saturday, right?"

"I wouldn't miss it for the world."

"Great, because Aunt Penny's really looking forward to finally meeting you."

Ashton heard a male voice in the background, and wondered who it belonged to.

"Baby, I have to go. The police just arrived to take Sienna's statement, and she wants me to sit in on the interview with her."

"No problem. Call me later. It doesn't matter how late. I need to know that you're okay."

"I will. Thanks for understanding, Ashton. My ex never showed any interest in the foundation, and he rolled his eyes whenever I tried to talk about my problems at work, so your support means the world to me."

"Haley, we're a team. Never forget that. I got your back, and I always will," he said, and hung up.

Ashton was bummed about not seeing Haley, but it was nothing a good, hard workout session in his home gym couldn't cure. After, he'd put on the Firebirds game, eat some ribs and then catch up on paperwork in his home office. Changing his mind about taking a shower, Ashton put his clothes back on, and picked his cell phone off the bed.

As he made his way out to the grill, he stopped dead in his tracks before the French doors. Damn. For the second time in minutes, his good mood fizzled. His parents were still sitting on the deck, and worse yet, they were eating the food he'd spent hours cooking for Haley.

Ashton cursed. There was no escaping his parents tonight, and although he was a successful businessman worth millions he suddenly felt like a prisoner in his own home.

Chapter 16

Ashton parked his Bugatti Veyron at the shopping plaza across the street from Regency Condominiums, stepped out of the driver's seat and strode around the hood of the car. Staring out of the windshield, Haley noticed everyone in the parking lot was staring at them. She felt embarrassed arriving at the grocery store in a fancy Italian sports car that cost more than her condo, but she stepped out of the vehicle with her head held high, took Ashton's hand and followed him inside the store.

Twenty minutes later, they left Winn-Dixie carrying plastic bags filled with fresh produce, organic food and knitting magazines. Not only had Ashton insisted on paying for the groceries Haley was picking up for Aunt Penny, he'd also purchased a lavish floral arrangement from the adjacent florist.

Crossing the street at the intersection, they chatted about their work week and their plans for the weekend. At Ashton's request, she'd packed an overnight bag and was looking forward to spending some quality time with him. He asked her about Sienna, and listened as Haley vented about her tense, hour-long meeting with Ms. Larimore that morning. Ashton told her what to do legally to help Sienna, and gave her tips for winning over the teen's mother as well. Haley doubted it would work—not when the single mother was in denial about her live-in boyfriend—but for the sake of Sienna, she was willing to give it a shot.

"Thanks, Ashton. I can always count on you to give me great advice."

"Anytime," he said, with a wink, and a grin.

Goose bumps tickled her skin.

"Can I ask you a personal question?" he asked.

Curious, Haley met his gaze, then slowly nodded her head.

"Did your aunt like your ex-boyfriend?" Ashton asked, a pensive expression on his face. "Did she think you guys were well suited for each other?"

"Yes, initially, but when he started mistreating me, she stopped inviting him to Sunday dinner and threatened to disown me if I continued dating him."

"I'm glad you dumped him. You deserve the best, and nothing less."

They shared a smile, and Haley sighed inwardly. Ashton was the best boyfriend she'd ever had, and every moment they spent together was a cherished memory.

"I appreciate you coming with me to see my aunt today. I know your friends probably gave you a hard time for missing the Firebirds game this afternoon, but I want you to know this means a lot to me. Aunt Penny is more than just a good friend. She's my family, and I value her opinion."

"Is that your way of telling me to be on my best behavior?"

"Yes," she said with a laugh. "Be good, Ashton."

"I will, but when we get back home it's on like Donkey Kong." Chuckling, he lowered his face to hers and brushed his mouth against the curve of her ear. "We're getting down and dirty tonight, and all weekend long."

Haley winked. "Promise?"

Laughing, they continued up the block, soaking in the radiant sunshine.

As they entered Regency Condominiums, Ashton's cell buzzed, and he stopped to read his newest text message. Haley hoped the loquacious doorman wasn't on duty, but when she strode inside the lobby, Matheus was the first person she saw. His face lit up, and he jogged over.

"Haley, I haven't seen you in a while. Where have you been hiding?" Wetting his lips with his tongue, he allowed his lascivious gaze to crawl slowly and purposely down her hips. "Damn, you're looking hot in that dress."

Appearing at her side, Ashton curled an arm around Haley's waist. "Good afternoon."

The grin slid off the doorman's face, and fear flashed in his eyes. "Y-y-you're Ashton Rollins," he stammered. "It's a pleasure to meet you, sir. Welcome to Regency Condominiums."

Ashton wore a polite smile, then gestured to the elevator. It was jam-packed, filled with couples, families and suit-class businessmen yammering on their cell phones, but Ashton ushered her inside. "Damn. Men flock to you everywhere we go," he complained, slowly shaking his head. "You're more popular than T-Swizzle, and she's an international pop star."

Haley cracked up, noticed everyone in the elevator was staring at her and clamped her lips together to trap a giggle inside her mouth. "What do you know about Taylor Swift? You're a chief operating officer at an aeronautics company, not one of her die-hard fans."

"I know she's got nothing on you. You're the most dynamic woman I have ever met."

"You're *such* a charmer," she said, giving him a peck on the cheek. "And I love it."

Exiting the elevator on the ninth floor, Haley linked arms with Ashton and led him down the hallway. She heard classical music playing and the distant sound of *Wheel of Fortune*, and wondered if Aunt Penny was watching her favorite game show on full blast again.

"I'm nervous," Ashton confessed with a sheepish smile. "What if Aunt Penny doesn't like me?"

"Then I'll have to find a new aunt, because you're definitely a keeper."

"I love when you quote me," he said. "It makes me feel so smart."

"That's because you are. And you're hot, too. *Muy caliente*, baby!"

Ashton pressed his mouth to hers, devouring her lips with his own. Desperate for more of him, Haley put her bags on the floor and draped her arms around his neck. Pressing her body flat against his, she moaned inside his mouth when she felt his erection against her thighs.

Desire heated her skin and before she knew what happened, she was lost in the moment, in the feel of Ashton. She stroked the back of his head, his shoulders and his chest. His dress shirt was a hindrance, a barrier she wanted to get rid of, but before she could unbutton it, she remembered they were in an apartment hallway, not Ashton's bedroom.

"Haley, dear, is that you carrying on?"

Haley's eyes flew open. Breaking off the kiss, she peered over Ashton's shoulder to see Aunt Penny standing in the doorway of her apartment with her hands on her hips. Haley wondered how much her aunt had seen and heard. Once she started kissing Ashton, there was just no stopping her. Her desire for him knew no bounds, and the more time they spent together the more she craved him. Like right now. Thoughts of making love to him consumed her, so she shook her head to clear her mind and straightened her crooked dress.

Haley wiped her lipstick off Ashton's mouth with her thumb, then winked at him. "Baby, let's go," she whispered, retrieving the grocery bags at her feet. "It's showtime."

Haley greeted Aunt Penny with a kiss on the cheek, then introduced Ashton.

"Ms. Washington, this is for you," he said, offering the flowers. "I hope you like them."

"Thank you, son." Aunt Penny closed her eyes, buried her nose in the bouquet and took a deep breath. "I love oriental lilies. They've always been my favorite flower. They typify beauty and elegance, and as you can see that's me in a nutshell."

The elderly woman laughed, and Ashton wore a broad smile.

"I couldn't agree more, Ms. Washington. Haley told me how you helped raise her and encouraged her to follow her dreams, so it's an honor to meet you. She's a very special woman."

Aunt Penny beamed. "What a lovely thing for you to say, but I can't take all of the credit. Her parents raised her well, and even as a little girl Haley had a kind, sweet temperament."

"She still does. I've never met a more considerate, compassionate person, and I feel fortunate to have Haley in my life. Meeting her has changed me for the better."

Moved by his words, Haley met his gaze and returned his smile.

"Come on in. I'll fix you two kids a snack. After all that kissing, I bet you're starving."

"Are you sure?" Ashton asked. "We don't want to interrupt your resting time."

"I'm not resting. I'm watching *Sons of Anarchy*. Outstanding show."

Haley saw Ashton's eyes widen, and knew he was shocked. Swallowing a laugh, she followed her aunt inside the apartment, and put the grocery bags on the kitchen counter.

"Ashton, have a seat in the living room," Aunt Penny instructed. "I'll be right there."

Nodding, he exited the kitchen and took a seat on the brown suede sofa.

"Honey, do me a favor." Aunt Penny shoved the bouquet into Haley's hands. "Put the lilies in a vase while I visit with your new gentleman friend."

Panic surged inside Haley's body. The fear in her heart must have shown on her face because Aunt Penny patted her forearm and told her Ashton was in good hands.

"Don't worry. I don't bite," she joked with a laugh.

"What are you going to talk to him about?"

"I'm going to pick his brain about lucrative business ventures in and around the Miami area, and find out what his intentions are toward my favorite niece, of course."

A smile curled her lips. "Aunt Penny, I'm not really your niece."

"But I love you like one, which is all the more reason for me to learn what his plans are." Fervently nodding her head, she clutched Haley's shoulders and steered her across the room. "Dear, hurry up and put the flowers into a vase. I don't want them to dry out."

For the next thirty minutes, Haley put away the groceries and cleaned out the pantry, all the while keeping an eye on Aunt Penny and Ashton. It was nerve-racking, only being able to hear bits and pieces of their conversation, and her heart stopped every time she heard her name. She was afraid of what Ashton was enduring, but when she finally brought a tray filled with coffee and pastries into the living room, she couldn't help but notice the amused expression on his face.

"What did I miss?" Haley asked, taking a seat on the couch. "What's so funny?"

Ashton held up his hands, and Haley groaned out loud. "Aunt Penny, not my childhood photo albums!"

Aunt Penny made her eyes wide. "What? Don't blame me. *He* asked."

"Why didn't you tell me you used to be a Girl Scout?" Ashton said. "You look adorable in your uniform, and check out all of your badges. You must have been the LeBron James of your troop!"

"She sure was." Aunt Penny wore a proud smile. "In less than three years, Haley received over forty badges for skills such as leadership, survival, water safety and first aid."

"So, if we got stranded in the middle of nowhere you'd know what to do?"

"Of course," Haley said, fervently nodding her head. "I'm a decorated Girl Scout who loves camping and the great outdoors, so you'd be in good hands."

Ashton kissed her forehead, and Haley snuggled against his shoulder as he talked to Aunt Penny. Like her, he had a small circle of friends, choosing to spend his free time with a few loved ones rather than a big crowd. Listening to him speak about his childhood and his strong bond with his mom, Haley was touched. He was open and honest about his feelings—crediting his mother for his professional success—and the more he spoke about her the wider Aunt Penny's smile grew.

Haley thought of her parents. She wished she saw them more often, but she didn't have time to travel to Pensacola. Her mom was hosting Thanksgiving dinner, and Haley was looking forward to going home for the holidays. She wanted Ashton to come with her and hoped Aunt Penny would be well enough to make the trip in November as well.

The sound of Aunt Penny's voice interrupted her musings.

"You've been so busy the last couple weeks, Haley, we haven't had a chance to talk about your trip to Venezuela. How was it? Did you kids have a good time? What was the best part?"

"Aunt Penny, it was amazing. We explored museums and art galleries, dined at incredible restaurants, spent the day hiking at Angel Falls, and even learned how to samba."

"No, *Haley* learned to samba, and *I* tried not to fall flat on my face." Ashton wore a sheepish smile. "I'm good at a lot of things, Ms. Washington, but dancing isn't one of them."

Everyone laughed, and Haley realized she'd been worried for nothing. Ashton was a great conversationalist, and her aunt was enjoying his company. Add to that, he had a big heart. Yesterday, as Haley was chairing the monthly staff meeting in the conference room, deliverymen from her favorite Italian restaurant had showed up with lunch. Needless to say, her staff had been overjoyed, and when she'd called Ashton to thank him he'd been humble and sweet.

Ashton draped an arm around her shoulders, and warmth spread through Haley's body. Never in her wildest dreams had she imagined that she'd meet a man as sincere and loving as Ashton. And when Aunt Penny winked at her, Haley knew she approved of Ashton, too. Having her aunt's blessing was the best feeling in the world.

Chapter 17

"You're dating Ashton Rollins?" Melinda Adams asked, a note of anger in her shrill, high-pitched voice. "Why am I always the last person to know what's happening in your life? Why won't you confide in me? I'm your mother, for goodness' sake!"

Haley stood inside Ashton's gourmet kitchen, holding her cell to her ear, her eyes wide, her mouth agape. A cold sweat drenched her skin, but she remained calm. "Who told you?"

"I called Aunt Penny and she let it slip that you and Ashton were at her apartment last weekend," she explained. "Is it true you're dating one of the most eligible and successful bachelors in Miami, or is Aunt Penny making up stories again?"

Needing a moment to organize her thoughts, Haley picked up her glass and sipped her orange juice. Her mom had a million questions about Ashton and his influential family, but Haley didn't answer them. Ashton's kitchen wasn't the right place to have a heart-to-heart talk with her mom, but tomorrow, when she returned home, she'd call Melinda and tell her all about her wonderful new boyfriend.

Her gaze strayed to the contemporary wall clock hanging above the walk-in pantry, and her eyes widened. Where had the time gone? They'd slept in that morning and had had a late breakfast in the outdoor living room, followed by yoga in Ashton's home gym. Her body tingled when she thought about their hour-long workout session. One kiss had led to another, and before Haley knew what was happening they were lying face-to-face on his yoga mat, buck naked, making love as if their lives depended on it. He'd climbed on top of her, positioned his erection between her legs and plunged so deep inside her she'd screamed in pleasure.

"Tell me everything, Haley. I'm sick of being in the dark. I deserve to know the truth."

Breaking free of her erotic thoughts, Haley turned on the faucet and washed the mixing bowls soaking in the sink. They were going to the symphony with Ashton's parents tonight, and if she wanted to be ready on time she had to hustle. Or suffer his mother's wrath when the limousine arrived at five o'clock. Ashton was upstairs in his office, hard at work reading contracts and answering emails, and Haley wanted to bring him a snack before she went to take a shower.

"Mom, I can't talk right now," she said, grabbing the baseball-themed oven mitts off the breakfast bar and putting them on. "I'll call you tomorrow night."

"No," Melinda argued. "I won't let you brush me off this time. I'm your mother and I have a right to know who you're dating, so spill the tea or I'll be on the next flight to Miami."

Raising an eyebrow, Haley stared down at her cell, confused by her mother's words. She suspected her mom was bluffing—Melinda hated airplanes and rarely traveled—but since she couldn't risk her mom showing up in Miami, searching Fisher Island for Ashton's estate, she took a deep breath and forced the truth out of her mouth. "Mom, it's true," she said, unable to wipe the smile off her lips. "I'm dating Ashton Rollins."

Her mother was silent so long Haley wondered if they'd lost the connection. She could hardly believe her mom was speechless.

"Ashton's a terrific guy who treats me well." Hearing the giddiness in her voice, Haley tempered her excitement. Melinda was a serious, no-nonsense woman who didn't believe in the concepts of soul mates or true love so she chose her words carefully. "I didn't tell you about Ashton initially because I thought it was too soon. I wanted to get to know him better and I have. He's a sensitive, loving man, and I have strong feelings for him."

"He's a little bit out of your league, don't you think?"

A sour taste filled Haley's mouth. *Thanks a lot*, she thought, saddened by her mother's words. *You always know what to say to make me feel like a winner.*

"Honey, no disrespect to you, because you're a lovely young woman with a great personality, but rich men usually date models and Hollywood starlets, not nonprofit workers who grew up on the wrong side of the tracks."

"Ashton's different," she bragged, allowing her mother's words to go in one ear and out the other. "He cares more about who I am as a person than about my physical measurements, and I love him for it. Ashton's unlike anyone I've ever met, and even though we're from two completely different worlds I think we have what it takes to have a long, lasting relationship."

Cradling her cell between her ear and her shoulder, Haley opened the oven, took out the pans and put them on top of the stainless-steel stove. A savory aroma sweetened the air, and her mouth watered at the scent of homemade beef jerky and chocolate chip cookies.

"I'm glad you're happy," Melinda said. "But don't rush into anything."

"Don't worry, Mom, we're not eloping to Vegas anytime soon!"

Haley laughed, but her mom didn't.

"Honey, I'm worried you won't be accepted by Ashton's well-heeled friends and family, but the whole thing is like such a Cinderella story that I hope I'm proven wrong."

You and me both, Haley thought, gazing out the floor-to-ceiling windows overlooking the backyard. They offered spectacular views of the turquoise-blue ocean and the city of Miami. Birds flew in the night sky, and the palm trees dotting the estate swayed in the breeze. "Mom, if it's okay with you, I'd like to bring Ashton to Thanksgiving dinner."

Haley held her breath. She thought of telling Melinda that Ashton had said the "M" word last night in bed, but changed her mind. It was a bad idea. She worried it would inevitably backfire in her face if she told her mom Ashton wanted to marry her, so she wisely kept her mouth shut.

"Do you think you'll be dating in two months' time?" Melinda asked quietly. "From what I read online, Ashton Rollins has a revolving door of celebrity girlfriends, and I don't want you to get hurt when things go south."

"Mom, they won't. Be positive for once. Everything's going to work out fine."

"For your sake, I hope I'm wrong, but my gut feeling is that Ashton's going to break your heart. Wealthy, successful men with an eye for the ladies *never* commit—"

Tired of her mom's negativity, Haley interrupted her midsentence and said, "Mom, I have to go, but we'll talk soon. Love you. Bye!"

Ending the call, Haley, tossed her cell on the counter.

Sadness coursed through her veins, making her feel low. It bothered her that her own mother didn't think she was good enough for Ashton. Her mother's words stung, but Haley decided not to dwell on them. Sure, she loved her mom, but she wasn't going to let Melinda or anyone else badmouth Ashton.

Her cell phone rang, and hope surged in her heart. Could it be her mom calling back to apologize? But when Haley saw her dad's number on the screen her shoulders sagged. The timing of his call wasn't a coincidence. No doubt Melinda had called Russell, told him about Ashton, and now he was calling to scold her. No thanks. Like her mom, her dad despised wealthy people, and Haley wouldn't be surprised if he told her to dump Ashton.

It's not going to happen, Haley thought, fervently shaking her head. *Sorry, Dad, this is my life, not yours, and I won't let you control me.*

Deciding to return his call tomorrow, Haley hit the decline button, filled a silver tray with the homemade treats and exited the kitchen. As she walked to Ashton's office, she took in the eye-catching artwork and imported Italian furniture. The Venetian glass chandeliers and marble flooring throughout the opulent mansion gleamed and sparkled.

After last night Haley's arms were sore and her feet ached, but she climbed the staircase to the second floor, eager to see Ashton. Last night, after the movie premiere of Will Smith's new action flick at Tower Theater, they'd joined Ashton's friends at La Mexicana for drinks. The celebrity hotspot was filled with spicy aromas, vibrant murals and glamorous A-list diners decked out in designer threads and bling. The restaurant had world-class food and breathtaking views of Biscayne Bay, but the highlight of Haley's night was dirty dancing with Ashton in the adjacent lounge. For hours, they'd flirted and kissed and danced, and for as long as Haley lived she'd never forget how desirable he'd made her feel. It didn't matter that his friends were watching: he'd lavished her with love and affection.

Walking down the hallway, Haley heard music playing and frowned. When had Ashton started listening to pop music? Was he actually singing along? Amused by his off-key rendition of Taylor Swift's latest hit, she knocked on his office door, then eased it open with her foot.

Her gaze landed on Ashton sitting behind his executive desk, and her heart swooned inside her chest. He was so handsome it was nearly impossible for her not to drool all over her denim shirtdress. They'd made love last night, and again that morning after their yoga session, but it obviously wasn't enough. Her nipples hardened under her bra, and every inch of her body—from her ears to her toes—craved his touch. If Haley didn't have to get ready for the symphony, she'd be all over him, but since she was scared of getting on his mother's bad side she struck the thought from her mind.

"I thought you could use a snack," Haley said, sailing through his spacious office.

"Perfect timing." Ashton took off his reading glasses and put them down on the desk. "I just finished reviewing the monthly financial statements, and I could use a break."

Bright, sunny and modern, the office was decorated with pendant lamps, plush, velvet couches, a colorful rug and Moroccan end tables. The wallpaper behind the desk was a blown-up antique map, and mounted shelves held aviation books and framed photographs. He'd never taken a bad picture, and Haley enjoyed admiring photographs of Ashton visiting Seattle's Museum of Flight, riding an elephant in Thailand and posing on a jet ski. Souvenirs of his overseas travels were prominently displayed on his desk, along with the copper sculptures she'd bought him at the open-air market in Caracas. Seeing them filled her mind with warm memories.

"I made all of your favorites." Haley put the tray on the round table positioned in front of the window, and gestured to a leather chair. "Baby, come eat before it gets cold."

From his desk, Ashton sniffed the air. "What is that delicious smell?"

"Homemade beef jerky, chocolate chip cookies and Turkish coffee, of course."

Love shone in his eyes, and a boyish grin curled his mouth. "Will you marry me?"

Haley burst out laughing. "Is that all it takes to win your heart? A home-cooked meal?"

"There are a couple *other* things you could do to seal the deal—"

Ashton's cell rang, and he broke off speaking. As he looked at the screen, his grin faded.

"Who is it?" Haley asked, curious to know who had ruined his good mood.

"My dad, and it's the third time he's called this afternoon." Raking a hand through his hair, Ashton released a deep, troubled sigh. "There's a problem with one of the designs on our new navigation system for the Boeing 747, and he expects me to fix it ASAP, but there's nothing I can do about it until Monday."

"Talk to your dad. I'll come back later."

Haley turned to leave, but Ashton seized her arm and pulled her down onto his lap.

"You're not going anywhere." He spoke in a stern, authoritative voice, but his gaze was full of warmth. "We're spending quality time together, and nothing matters more to me than getting you out of this dress and into my bed."

Aroused by his words, Haley straddled his lap and linked her hands around his neck.

Desire burned inside her, and all she could think about was making love to Ashton. He made her feel cherished and adored, as if she was the only person in the world who mattered, and it was a remarkable feeling. She wanted to please him, and knew just what to do to turn him on.

Licking the rim of his ear with her tongue, she pressed her breasts against his chest, and tenderly stroked the back of his head. "Who needs a bed when we're nice and cozy right here?" she whispered in a sultry voice. "I've always fantasized about making love on a desk."

His mouth moved across hers, ever so slowly, and tingles danced along her spine. He kissed her neck, right below her ear, and Haley tilted her head to give him better access. She wanted more. Needed more. Wanted to make love to him right then and there, before they ran out of time.

Lost in the moment, Haley closed her eyes as Ashton kissed her, his tongue swirling around her mouth. He tasted delicious, better than dark chocolate, and his thick, scrumptious lips thrilled her. His kiss was slow and thoughtful, but packed with heat. He didn't rush; instead he took his time pleasing and exploring her body with his mouth and hands.

Ashton unbuttoned her dress, slid it up over her shoulders, and dropped it on the floor. Swallowing hard, Haley squirmed on his lap. As he undid her bra, lust sparked in Ashton's eyes, and he slowly licked his lips, telling Haley that he desired her as much as she desired him. It was a heady feeling.

Showering her face with kisses, he moved his strong, warm hands over her hips and thighs. Her body was sensitive to his touch. On fire. So damn hot perspiration wet her skin. Haley had to have him. Here. Now. Before she lost complete control. It was just like last night in the bedroom. Ripping Ashton's suit from his body wasn't her finest moment, and every time she remembered what she'd done, shame burned her cheeks.

"I've never felt this way about anyone before. You're all I think about," he confessed.

Haley stilled, listened intently as he spoke. She didn't want to miss a single word.

"I can't get enough of you, baby. I want to make love to you every second of every day."

"Is knockin' boots *all* you think about?" she teased. Cupping his face in her hands, she gazed deep into his eyes. "What happened to that patient, understanding man I used to know who said he didn't care about sex, and wanted to get to know me better as person?"

"You rocked his world in Venezuela, and now he's addicted to you!" Ashton kissed the tip of her nose, her cheeks and the corners of her lips. "I'm weak for you, Haley. Don't you see that? I've fallen hard for you, and now I'm under your spell."

The sound of his deep, husky voice made Haley shudder. She was having an eargasm, tingling uncontrollably, suddenly unable to think or speak. His mouth continued its sensual assault, nibbling on her neck, her collarbone and the swell of her cleavage.

Haley took his hand, sucked his index finger into her open mouth, then pulled over her panties and slid it between her legs. It was a direct hit. A bull's eye. Desire shot through her veins, and excitement rippled across her skin. Parting her thighs, she welcomed him deeper inside her wet center. In-and-out, back-and-forth, she moved his fingers around her sex. Hungry for more, she pumped and swiveled her hips, panting and moaning his name.

Her passion mounted, consuming her. Haley couldn't stop the emotions swirling around her body and the tremors flooding her sex. Worse still, she couldn't control her thoughts. She wanted Ashton to be more aggressive, and when she parted her lips, every wicked and salacious thought fell out of her mouth. "That's it baby…right there. Harder…faster…deeper. Do me, baby!"

"Be patient," he said with a Cheshire-cat grin. "I have all night to please you."

"We're going to the symphony with your parents tonight, remember?" Haley said, panting her words. "A limousine will be here at five o'clock to pick us up."

"You're right. I forgot. We better make this quick."

"No. Don't. I want more… I need more."

"Is that right?" Ashton circled an erect nipple with his thumb. He kissed it, licked it, then sucked it into his open mouth. "I'm happy to oblige."

Instinctively, she cradled his head in her hands, stroked his hair, neck and shoulders.

He slid another finger between her legs. "What my baby wants, my baby gets."

Overcome, Haley pressed her eyes shut. Her pulse raced, and the muscles between her legs quivered. Rocking against him, she swiveled her hips. Pleasure flowed through her core, filling her to the brim. It was heaven. Nirvana. Still, Haley wanted more.

Desperate to have Ashton inside her, turning her out like only he could, Haley unbuckled his pants and captured his erection. She stroked his balls, massaging them gently. It didn't matter if they dated for years—her desire for him would never die. They'd clicked from the moment they met, and over the last six weeks their bond had only gotten stronger. Their lovemaking was exquisite, like something in a French movie, and Haley couldn't imagine ever being intimate with anyone else. He was it for her, the only man she wanted. He'd always have her heart—*and* her body.

Ashton crushed his mouth to hers, nipped and nibbled

on her bottom lip as if it was a piece of tropical fruit. He made her feel desirable, gave her the freedom to feel, not think, and with each slow, passionate kiss her ardor grew. His heavy breathing drowned out the John Legend song now playing on the stereo, but his deep, guttural groans were music to her ears. Knowing that she was pleasing him gave Haley an adrenaline rush.

Ashton dug his hands into her hair, played with her lush, thick locks. Pulling her toward him, he deepened their kiss. Haley couldn't think of anything but pleasing Ashton. It was a challenge staying in the moment, maintaining her composure, when all she wanted to do was scream and moan, but Haley conquered her emotions and tightened her hold around his neck.

In one swift motion, Ashton yanked aside her panties and thrust his erection inside her. He kissed her hard on the mouth, trapping an ear-shattering scream inside her mouth. He cupped her breasts, tweaked, then rubbed her nipples.

Gripping the back of his executive chair, Haley rotated her hips. Increasing her pace, she moved faster, pumped harder, until waves of pleasure radiated through her core. She didn't want their lovemaking to end. Not yet. She could stay in the office sexing Ashton for the rest of the night. Forget the symphony and dinner at a five-star restaurant in downtown Miami with his parents. He was all she needed. All she wanted. And that would never change.

Ashton picked her up, set her down on the desk in front of him and hiked her legs in the air. The depth of his penetration and the urgency of his stroke stole her breath. He was a world-class lover, the only man to ever blow her mind between the sheets. Haley had never seen this side of him and wondered if his ferocious lovemaking had anything to do with the rap song now playing on the stereo. Thrusting to the pulsing, hypnotic beat of the music, Ashton stroked and massaged her curves.

Flipping her onto her stomach, as if she was as light as a feather, Ashton palmed her ass in his hands. He squeezed it, slapped it, rubbed it, kissed each firm, supple cheek. It had never been like this. Ashton was the only man who'd ever possessed her mind, body and soul. Their connection was unlike anything she'd ever known.

What a difference a year made, Haley thought, rubbing her ass against his crotch. Before dating Ashton, she hadn't cared about sex. Never thought about it. Never craved it. Why would she? She'd only had one serious boyfriend, and their sex life had been mediocre at best. Unlike her ex, Ashton would rather give than receive, and he was such a passionate, selfless lover Haley wanted to make love to him every day. Dating Ashton had not only bolstered her sexual confidence, it had given her a fresh outlook on life. Haley was so hopeful and optimistic about their future that lately she had a permanent smile on her face. Thanks to Ashton she was a better CEO and a happier woman.

"Damn, Haley, you're killing me. I don't think I can last much longer."

Glancing over her shoulder, she met his eyes just before Ashton lowered his head for a kiss. His tongue explored her mouth, searching, thrilling, pleasing her, and his hands caressed her flesh.

"Don't stop. Please don't stop," she begged, her low, throaty voice sounding foreign to her ears. "I love the way you make me feel, Ashton. I love this… I love you."

Shock registered on his face, then a smile crept over his lips. "What did you just say?"

Haley opened her mouth, but electricity struck her body like a lightning bolt. The room spun around her, and radiant, vibrant colors exploded behind her eyes. It was the most powerful orgasm she'd ever experienced, and the sheer intensity of it caused Haley to collapse on the desk, panting like a sprinter at the end of the one-hundred meter dash.

Ashton gathered her in his arms and kissed her forehead. Her thoughts cleared, and shame burned her cheeks. Floored by her confession, Haley couldn't speak. What had she done? What had she been thinking? *That's the problem*, she thought, dodging his piercing gaze. *I wasn't thinking.*

Standing on wobbly legs, Haley didn't know how she was going to make it to the master bedroom, let alone the symphony. She longed for a bubble bath and a power nap.

"You were saying, Ms. Adams?" Ashton asked her, standing up beside her. "Tell me again how much you love me."

An amused expression covered his face, and Haley knew he was having fun teasing her. Deciding two could play that game, she faked a yawn and shrugged a shoulder. "It was the alcohol talking," she said innocently. "I get chatty after a couple drinks, and I had several glasses of merlot at lunch."

It was a lie, and Haley could tell by Ashton's arched brows that he didn't believe her.

"Yeah, right," he scoffed. "You love me. Just admit it."

I do, baby, with all my heart, but I'm scared if I tell you the truth it will backfire in my face.

Ashton cupped her chin in his hands and caressed her skin softly with his thumb. "The heart's letter is read through the eyes, and it's obvious you love me as much and as deeply as I love you, so don't fight it. We're soul mates, and we're destined to be together."

Haley blinked back tears. She was so happy she thought she'd burst with joy. Jumping into Ashton's arms, she threw her hands around his neck, pulling him close. As they intertwined fingers and feasted on each other's lips, Haley fell even deeper in love.

Chapter 18

Ashton stuck his head inside the doorway of the master bathroom, took one look at Haley standing in front of the lighted, wall mirror in a purple, lace push-up bra, matching thong panties and leather, ankle-tie pumps, and decided to cancel their plans with his parents. Why would he want to go to Beethovenmania at the Miami Symphony when he could make love to the woman of his dreams for the rest of the night?

Aroused by the thought, Ashton plucked at his crisp, navy-blue dress shirt. Watching her lotion her legs with cocoa butter was a turn-on. The hairs on the back of his neck shot up, and an erection grew inside his slim-fitted pants. It poked at his zipper, dying for release.

Haley caught him staring at her, smiled sheepishly and raised a hand in the air. "Babe, I'll be ready in five minutes," she said, spraying Chanel No. 5 on the side of her neck. "All I need to do is slip on my gown, and I'm good to go."

A grin claimed Ashton's mouth. He'd bought the fragrance for Haley weeks earlier as a gift, and smelling the floral scent in the air made his mouth water. Coming up behind her, he slid his hands across her stomach, and pressed soft kisses along her neck. "Does that feel good?" he whispered, allowing his lips to linger on her skin. "Do you like that?"

Her eyes fluttered closed. "I don't like it. I *love* it."

"Do you want more?"

"Yes, please."

"Good. I'll call my parents, tell them something came up and apologize on your behalf." Cupping her breasts in his hands, he brushed his erection against her tight, firm ass. "We're spending the rest of the night in bed."

"Oh, no, we aren't," Haley quipped, adamantly shaking her head. "If you cancel on your parents they'll blame me, and I don't want to get on your mother's bad side."

"But, baby, I need you."

"Boy, don't even try it. We're going to the symphony with your parents, and that's final."

Ashton reached for her, but she spun around and braced her hands against his chest.

"What are you doing?" he asked, cocking an eyebrow.

"Kicking you out."

A chuckle burst out of his mouth. "You can't kick me out of my own bathroom."

"Yes, I can. I'm using it, so bounce." Haley gestured to the door with her head. "Hang out in the bedroom until I'm finished getting ready. I'm almost done."

"And if I don't?"

"Then you'll be sleeping alone tonight."

"All right, all right, I'm leaving." Wearing an innocent face, Ashton raised his hands in the air as if he was surrendering to the cops. "You don't have to play hardball. I'll behave."

Haley gave him a peck on the lips. Her breath was minty fresh, and one, chaste kiss wasn't enough. Ashton was so desperate for her he smothered her mouth with his own. Their tongues mated, teased and played. "You're so beautiful I can't take my eyes off you," he praised, inhaling her fragrant scent.

"Thanks, babe. You're beautiful, too."

Ashton chuckled, felt like a million bucks when Haley whistled and fanned her face.

"I swoon every time you look at me, and your kisses leave me breathless." Her tone had a hint of sexual innuendo, her come-hither look was hypnotic, and her dirty, little smile made his pulse race. "Now, scoot. I'll be right out."

"But I want to make love. It's all I can think about."

"Later. I promise."

Returning to the bedroom to finish watching the rest of the Firebirds game, Ashton grabbed the remote control off the entertainment unit and jacked up the volume. Rain fell from the sky, and the wind howled, wipping tree branches against the windows.

Ashton put his legs up on the leather ottoman. The décor in the master suite complemented his personality, and the serene blues and creams created a peaceful, relaxing atmosphere. Ashton heard his cell ring and unplugged it from the charger. When he saw the name on the screen, his first thought was to decline the call, but since he didn't want Joshua blowing up his cell phone for the rest of the night he reluctantly answered.

"Hello, Joshua, how are things?"

"Ashton, we need to talk. I have something important to tell you, and it can't wait."

Tuning Joshua out, he let his gaze stray to the bathroom door. From where Ashton was standing, he could see Haley fussing with her hair, and admired her stunning appearance. In her sequined ivory gown she was sophisticated and sexy, and she was sure to turn heads at the symphony.

His palms itched to touch her. Ashton couldn't wait to get his hands on her—or rather, *under* her dress. And he would, as soon as he got Joshua off the phone. They had thirty minutes until the limo arrived, and he was feenin' for a quickie.

"What is it?" he barked at Joshua. "I'm on my way out."

"Mia wasn't driving her car the night she died. You were."

Ashton stopped breathing. He didn't understand, couldn't make sense of what Joshua had just blurted out. He wanted to end the call, but instead of hanging up he pressed his cell closer to his ear and listened intently to what his nemesis was saying about Mia's tragic accident.

"I've uncovered irrefutable evidence of a cover-up," Joshua said.

What the hell? Ashton's heart beat was deafening, piercing his eardrum. It felt as if his silk Burberry tie was choking him, but his hands were shaking so hard he couldn't take it off. *This can't be happening*, Ashton thought, at a loss for words. *Joshua is lying. He's trying to steal the presidency from me. That's why he's making up stories. To rattle me. To get under my skin, but I won't let him.*

"The officer who arrived first on the scene that night was ordered to falsify his report," Joshua stated in a clear, calm voice. "I have proof that your father paid Lieutenant Bale to make the problem go away."

A searing pain spread through Ashton's chest. Nothing was adding up. Struggling to separate fact from fiction, he paused to consider everything his dad had told him about the accident. A prisoner of his thoughts, he relived the conversation they'd had at the hospital when he had regained consciousness. Ashton had to be honest with himself. He had no recollection of the car accident, but the story his dad had told him hadn't made sense. Still didn't, ten years later.

Could it be true? Was it his fault that Mia had died? *Why can't I remember?* A cold chill stabbed his spine. The walls closed in around him, started to crumble at his feet. If what Joshua was saying was true, his father had lied to him. Deceived him. Betrayed him. But why? Why had Alexander paid off the cops? Why hadn't his dad told him the truth? What other secrets was his father hiding?

Crushed by the weight of his despair, he felt his knees buckle, and he sank onto the bed. "I—I—I have to go," Ashton stammered, rubbing at his eyes.

The room spun out of control, and his vision blurred. It was hard to think, to make sense of everything Joshua had told him, and Ashton feared he was going to get sick.

Ending the call, Ashton chucked his cell on the bed, and dropped his face in his hands.

"Baby, I'm ready," Haley chirped in a singsong voice. "What do you think? Do I look sophisticated enough to attend the Miami Symphony with the esteemed Rollins family?"

Her words turned to garble in his ears, and for the first time ever Ashton wished Haley wasn't at his estate. He'd never spoken to her about Mia's death and didn't want to. It wasn't the kind of topic that came up in casual conversation, and after years of silence from his family, he'd gotten into the habit of keeping everything about that tragedy bottled up inside.

"Ashton, baby, what's wrong? Why are you upset?"

Upset was an understatement, he thought, clenching his fists.

Sitting down beside him on the bed, Haley gently rubbed his neck and shoulders. Her touch was warm and soothing, but it didn't alleviate the tension in his body. Ashton had never felt more helpless. He didn't know how to process the information Joshua had shared with him.

"Talk to me, Ashton. Is it about the faulty navigation system you told me about?"

It took every ounce of courage Ashton had but he opened up to Haley about Mia's car accident. He told her his version of the events, without mentioning Joshua's accusation of his father's cover-up. "It's been ten years since Mia's death, and I know I should be over it by now, but not a day goes by that I don't miss her. She was special to me, and I'll never forget her."

"That must have been awful for you, losing your first love in such a tragic way," she said quietly, moving even closer to him on the bed. "I can't imagine what you've been through."

"My dad told me Mia was driving."

A frown bruised her lips. "You don't believe him? Why not?"

"I should have trusted my instincts." Standing, he paced the length of the bedroom, voicing his thoughts. "It didn't make any sense to me at the time, because I always drove when we went out on dates, and now Joshua has proof that my dad lied…"

Ashton trailed off, unable to finish his thought. Embarrassed and ashamed about the things his father had done, he couldn't bear to tell Haley what Joshua had told him on the phone minutes earlier. The lump in his throat grew, and his eyes filled with unshed tears. Not because he was scared of losing everything but because his father had deceived him. Mia's death had destroyed him, but it was his father's betrayal that cut deep.

He turned to Haley. "You should go. I'm not fit to be anyone's boyfriend."

Her lips parted in surprise, and a pained expression

flashed across her face. "Ashton, I meant what I said earlier. I love you, and I'll always be here for you."

He shook his head. "I need some space right now. I want to be alone."

"What about our plans with your parents?"

"Screw them," he shot back. "They lied to me, and I don't want to see them."

"You don't mean that. You're just upset."

Ashton kicked the bronze lampstand so hard it crashed to the floor. The bulb shattered, and the popping sound made Haley jump. "Don't tell me how I feel," he shouted, voicing his anger. "You don't know the hell they've put me through."

His cell phone rang, and he glanced toward the king-sized bed. Fear rooted his feet to the floor, making it impossible for him to move. What if it was Joshua again? A knot formed in his stomach. What if he had more damning information? Or worse, what if Lieutenant Bale was calling to corroborate the story? Like a freight train zipping down the tracks, Ashton's thoughts derailed, jumped from one theory to the next.

"I want to help." Standing, Haley crossed the room toward him, a sympathetic expression on her face. "We can get through this."

Ashton stuck his hands into his pockets.

"Please don't push me away," she whispered.

"Dammit, this isn't about you." He jabbed a finger at his chest. "It's about me."

Haley reached for him, but he shied away from her touch.

"I'll get your things." His mind made up, Ashton marched into the walk-in closet, grabbed her leather tote bag and returned to the bedroom. "I'll see you out."

"No. Don't," she said softly, shaking her head. "I know the way."

They stood in silence, staring at each other for several seconds, and all Ashton could think was, *Please go. Please don't make this harder on me than it already is.* Her bottom lip quivered, but she straightened her shoulders, picked up her bag and fled the master bedroom.

Ashton hung his head. Instead of feeling relieved that Haley was gone he felt a profound sense of loss, as if he was all alone in the world. And he was. His parents had lied to him, some of the Millionaire Moguls were plotting against him, and Haley—the woman he loved more than life itself—was gone forever, and he had no one to blame but himself.

Chapter 19

"The National Weather Service has just issued a weather advisory for Miami," the female news reporter said. "Meteorologists are predicting a tropical storm with heavy rain and strong winds."

Haley turned off the car radio. She didn't need that meteorologist telling her she was in the midst of a wicked storm. Besides, she'd had enough bad news for one day. Ashton's words played in her mind, wounding her afresh. *I need some space... You should go... I want to be alone.*

Tears slid down her cheeks and splashed onto her designer gown. Ashton had bought it for her days earlier while shopping at the Miami Design District, and remembering how much fun they'd had making out in the fitting room made her heart sad. Three hours ago she was making love to Ashton in his office, and now they were over. How had things ended up like this? she wondered, releasing a deep sigh. Why had he pushed her away? Didn't he know how much she loved him? Needed him? Haley wasn't the type to give up, and never accepted "no" for an answer, but she knew when it was time to throw in the towel with Ashton. He didn't want her at his estate, and she wasn't going to stay where she wasn't welcome.

Wiping her eyes with the back of her hand, Haley struggled to make sense of what had happened. Hurt by Ashton's cold and callous behavior, she felt an overwhelming urge to cry, and bit down on her bottom lip to keep the tears at bay. He'd made her feel small, insignificant, as if he didn't care about her, and his rejection stung. A painful realization dawned on her. Her mom was right: Ashton didn't love her.

Swallowing hard to alleviate the lump in her throat, Haley peered out the windshield. It was raining so hard her windshield wipers couldn't keep up with the downpour. How fitting. The bleak weather matched her mood. Debris flew in the air, and she passed downed power lines and uprooted trees.

Haley was driving below the speed limit, but it was hard to maneuver her car through the flooded streets. The fast-moving storm was wreaking havoc on the city, and Haley feared she wouldn't make it home in one piece.

Stopped at the intersection, Haley grabbed her cell from the center console to dial Becca's number, when her thoughts took another turn. Aunt Penny! Suddenly, concern shifted from herself and her friend to the older woman. Did she have working flashlights? A three-day survival kit prepared?

Haley put on her turn signal and switched lanes. As she turned onto Seventh Avenue, headlights flashed in her eyes through the pouring rain, blinding her momentarily. She heard horns blare and jerked the car to the right, out of oncoming traffic. She felt the car jolt as it went up over the curb, onto the sidewalk and right into a tree.

Shaken up, Haley waited for her thoughts to clear. She

dropped her hands in her lap and took a deep, calming breath. It didn't help. Her mouth was so dry she couldn't swallow, and her limbs were shaking. Could this night get any worse? First Ashton had kicked her out, then she'd gotten caught in a tropical storm and now she'd damaged her car. *What else can go wrong tonight?*

Left with no other options, Haley realized she'd have to walk the rest of the way to Aunt Penny's. She rooted around the backseat till she found a raincoat she'd stashed there weeks ago and put it on. When she got out of the car, the blustery breeze whipped her hair around her face. Haley wanted to inspect the front bumper for damage but she was afraid the wind would blow her away. She focused on putting one foot in front of the other, moving slowly down the street toward Aunt Penny's condo. She wished she'd changed her clothes before leaving Ashton's house. But there'd been no time.

He'd wanted her gone, and Haley didn't want to overstay her welcome.

Approaching Regency Condominiums, Haley noticed the building was pitch-black.

Worried about Aunt Penny's well-being, she ran toward the entrance. The front door swung open, and someone yanked her inside the darkened lobby.

"Haley, what are you doing here?" Matheus asked, a bewildered expression on his face. He was holding a flashlight in one hand and a walkie-talkie in the other. "It's a tropical storm. The power is out across the city. It's not safe to be out on the streets."

Trembling, her teeth chattering, water dripping down her face and her clothes sticking to her body, Haley stepped away. "I need to check on Aunt Penny. I'm worried about her being alone during the storm."

"Is Mr. Rollins with you?"

Shaking her head, Haley lowered her gaze to the floor so Matheus wouldn't see the tears in her eyes. Memories of her and Ashton's afternoon tryst consumed her mind, and her body tingled in remembrance of his warm caress. She banished the memory and focused on the problem at hand. "Do you have an extra flashlight I can use?"

"No problem. I'll escort you upstairs."

Mentally and physically drained, she needed all her strength to climb the stairs to the ninth floor, and by the time she reached Aunt Penny's apartment she was panting. She took off her raincoat and, thanking the doorman for his help, used the spare key to unlock the door. She went inside, hung up her coat and followed the sound of the radio to the living room, where she found Aunt Penny sitting calmly in her favorite chair, working on her latest knitting project by candlelight. She mustered a smile. "Hi, Aunt Penny."

"Haley, what a pleasant surprise," she said in a cheery voice. "I wasn't expecting to see you tonight. You're supposed to be at the symphony with Ashton and his parents, no?"

Feeling her eyes tear, she couldn't speak.

"Haley, what's wrong? Why are you crying?"

Sniffling, Haley wiped at her eyes.

"Come here." Aunt Penny stood, her arms outstretched, and spoke in a soft, soothing voice. "Tell me all about it."

She hugged Haley, gently stroking her wet, matted hair, and Haley broke down. She couldn't hold it together anymore. She had a good, hard cry. She thought she was coming to her aunt's rescue but in fact it was Aunt Penny who was saving her right now.

She told the woman what had happened, pouring out her feelings. "I'm so confused right now. What should I do?"

"That depends. Do you love Ashton, or are you friends with benefits?"

"Aunt Penny!" she teased, giving the woman a knowing look. "What do *you* know about friends with benefits? You're eighty-eight years old."

"I know plenty. I watch HBO!"

The women laughed, drowning out the noise of the battery-operated radio.

"I love Ashton, and I know he loves me. That's why I'm so confused by his behavior."

"It sounds like he's going through a rough time right now, and it seems to me that once the circuits are restored you should call him. Nothing can stand in the way of true love."

Hope flowed through Haley's body. Aunt Penny's words resonated with her, touching the depths of her soul. Reminded her how much Ashton meant to her, and how strong their bond was. Their relationship was worth fighting for. *He* was worth fighting for. And the next time she saw him, she was going to tell him everything that was in her heart.

Haley opened her eyes to daylight. Looking around, she realized she'd dozed off on Aunt Penny's living room couch last night while they were talking. She snuggled under the thermal blanket. Losing Ashton was a bitter and helpless feeling, and Haley longed to be back in his arms.

Vivid images and memories of him filled her mind. Thinking about all the good times they'd shared made her hopeful about reconciling with him. And she would. They were soulmates, and she wasn't going to throw their relationship away after one argument.

Yawning, she tossed aside her blanket and dragged herself up from the couch. She glanced out the window, surprised to see how clear the sky was. The storm clouds were gone, and the sun was shining bright, promising another hot, summer day. Haley spotted her purse at the foot of the couch and rummaged around inside for her cell. As expected, it was dead. She looked around and saw no power to any of the lights or electrical equipment and knew she'd have to charge it later.

At the end of the hallway, Haley peeked into Aunt Penny's bedroom. Asleep in her canopy bed, surrounded by fluffy, white pillows, the older woman looked peaceful and content. Thanks to Aunt Penny's advice, Haley knew what to do to help Ashton. Once the power was restored, she'd call him and this time she wouldn't let him push her away. They needed each other, and Haley didn't want to live without him.

Thankful she had clothes and toiletries in the spare bedroom, Haley took a shower, blow-dried her hair and put on a floral-print sundress. Hearing a knock on the front door and fearing the noise would wake up Aunt Penny, she raced down the hallway. Last night Matheus had promised to bring her breakfast, but Haley wasn't in the mood for company. She needed to get her vehicle towed, get a rental car and get groceries for Aunt Penny. In addition to seeing Ashton today, she wanted to check up on Sienna. It was going to be a busy day for her, and the sooner she headed out the better.

Haley yanked open the door, and gasped. Ashton! Sweat glistened on his face, and he was breathing so hard she feared he'd collapse at her feet. They locked eyes, stared at each other for a long, nerve-racking moment, but Haley still couldn't believe he was standing on Aunt Penny's welcome mat. "Ashton, what are you doing here?"

"I freaked out when I couldn't find you at home."

Haley frowned. "You went to my house?"

"I couldn't imagine what you'd be doing out in the storm, but I had a feeling you might go check on Aunt Penny," he explained. "I remembered your aunt's address from my visit a few weeks back, and when I found your wrecked car I feared the worst."

Embarrassed that she'd crashed into a tree, Haley dodged his gaze and fiddled with her silver thumb ring. "It was nothing. Just a minor accident."

"I was so worried about you I abandoned my Ferrari and ran all the way here."

"That explains why you're out of breath."

Stepping forward, Ashton took her in his arms and held her tight. "We have a lot to discuss, but first and foremost, I love you and I never meant to hurt you."

"Then why did you kick me out of your house last night?"

"I was mad and confused and hurt but if I'd known about the storm I never would have asked you to leave. Haley, baby, I'm sorry."

"How do I know the next time you get pissed off you won't toss me out of your place?"

Ashton winced as if he had an infected tooth, then blew out a deep breath. "Because I'm man enough to admit I made a mistake, and I'm more committed to you than ever. I don't want to be alone. I want to be with you."

A door creaked open down the hall, and Haley noticed an elderly man with wiry hair watching them.

"Let's go inside," she said, taking his hand. "We'll have more privacy."

They sat down on the sofa, and as Ashton opened up to her about his phone conversation with Joshua last night, Haley noticed he was calm and composed. Still, she suspected he was torn up inside. He had to be. Eight hours ago his life had been turned upside down, and the dark circles under his eyes suggested he hadn't had any sleep.

"Do you think Josh is telling the truth?" Haley asked, blown away by his confession.

"He could be. I have no memory of the accident and I've always relied on my father's version of events, but what Joshua said makes sense to me. Mia never drove when we went out, so it's hard for me to believe she was behind the wheel that night. Furthermore, she didn't drink or do drugs so the police report must have been fabricated."

"What are you going to do?"

"Uncover the truth, once and for all, no matter what."

Deep down, Haley was worried about the potential fallout, but she kept her thoughts to herself. Ashton already had enough on his plate, and she didn't want to add to his stress.

"My only concern is how this scandal might affect the Millionaire Moguls and The Aunt Penny Foundation," he said, his voice tinged with sadness. "I think it's best for everyone if I resign as president and let Joshua take over."

Haley closed her gaping mouth. "But he was blackmailing you a few hours ago."

"There was no blackmail involved. Last night he came to me, man to man, trying to get the information to me discreetly. We spoke again this morning, and he promised not to leak the news to the press. I trust him. Unlike my father, he won't betray me."

"Do you think you could have been drinking that night, or under the influence of drugs?"

Ashton shook his head. "No way. I rarely drink, and I've never even smoked, let alone tried drugs. That's why I don't understand why my father would lie and say that Mia was driving. Even if I was behind the wheel, it was an accident. With my dad's team of illustrious lawyers, I probably would have gotten off scot-free. So why make up a story?"

A question rose in her thoughts, but before she could speak, Ashton did.

"I wonder if Mia had drugs in her system, or if this was another one of my father's lies." Pressing his eyes shut, he dragged a hand down the length of his face. "This is a nightmare."

"Don't worry. We'll get to the bottom of things. Together."

"We will? Are you sure you still want to be with me?"

The somber expression on his face pierced Haley's heart.

"I have a feeling things are going to get a lot worse before they get better," Ashton said, "and I don't want your name dragged through the mud because you're my girlfriend."

"I'm not going anywhere. It doesn't matter how bad things get, I'm not leaving you."

His eyes were filled with sadness, but a smile curled his lips. "Can I get that in writing?"

"No," she quipped, resting a hand on his cheek. "But I can prove it with a kiss."

"*Now* you're talking my language."

The warmth of his lips, and his tender caress along her arms and hips made heat flood her body. Ashton held her tight, whispering soft, sweet words in her ears, and Haley knew nothing would ever tear them apart again.

Chapter 20

Tuxedo-clad servers holding silver dessert trays moved around the backyard of Ashton's estate, offering guests champagne and decadent pastries flown in from his favorite New York bakery. Standing near the pool, chatting with his friends and associates about the stock market, Ashton took in the sights and sounds of the Prescott George seventy-fifth anniversary party. Hours earlier, guests had arrived at his Fisher Island estate in chauffeured limousines, and from the moment they'd set foot on his property they'd been treated like royalty. They'd enjoyed signature cocktails and appetizers, a scrumptious, seven-course meal prepared by a culinary genius, and a surprise performance from a world-renowned jazz singer. Representatives from Prescott George chapters all over the country were in attendance, and they praised him for throwing an impressive party.

Cheers rang out, drawing his attention across the yard, and Ashton chuckled. Angela Trainor and Becca Wright—who were both sporting sparkly engagement rings—were leading the dancing to an all-female R&B band. As expected, their adoring fiancés, Daniel Cobb and Joshua DeLong, were rooting them on. The starry night air was filled with music, laughter and boisterous conversation.

Pleased that the party was a hit, Ashton slid an arm around Haley's waist and hugged her to his side. It had been two weeks since the tropical storm, but it felt as if years had passed since he'd tracked her down at Aunt Penny's apartment and begged her for forgiveness. They were closer than ever, and if not for Haley's unconditional love and unwavering support he wouldn't have the courage to do what was right.

"This is the best charity event I've ever been to," Haley confessed, swaying her body to the beat of the music. "You Millionaire Moguls *really* know how to get down!"

His mouth watered when Haley swiveled her hips against his crotch. Her gold, backless dress had a stunning silhouette that showed off her slim waist, and all night he'd been stroking and caressing her smooth brown skin.

"I love this song," Haley said, doing a twirl. "Dance with me, baby."

Ashton glanced at his diamond wrist watch. "I have to go. It's time."

"Do you want me to come with you?"

"No, I'm good." Giving her a one-arm hug, he kissed the top of her forehead. "You being here tonight is enough. It means more to me than you'll ever know, and I love you for it."

His heart was hammering in his chest, but Ashton marched confidently through the backyard. As he took the stage, the music stopped, the band stepped aside and the fashionably dressed crowd exploded in cheers and applause.

"I want to thank everyone for coming to the seventy-fifth anniversary party of Prescott George." Ashton waited for the whistles and cheers to die down before he continued his speech.

"As for the Prescott George organization, there is going to be a change in the way things are run from here on out. The Moguls needs some new blood and fresh ideas. To achieve that goal, I'm suggesting there be copresidents from now on."

The rumble in the crowd reflected everyone's surprise, and the wide-eyed expression on his father's face made Ashton want to laugh, but he didn't. There was nothing funny about what his dad had done to him, and his hands clenched in fists when he remembered Alexander's lies.

"I will not be running for another term..."

Gasps filled the air, but he continued, full speed ahead.

"I'm nominating Joshua DeLong and Daniel Cobb as copresidents, and I hope you'll give them your full support because they're destined to do great things for this remarkable organization," he said with confidence, meaning every word. "Now, back to the party! The night's still young so dance, eat and drink some more!"

As Ashton exited the stage, he spotted his dad elbowing his way through the crowd.

The band returned to the stage, and when the lead singer ripped the microphone off the stand and belted out a Smokey Robinson classic the crowd went wild.

Alexander grabbed Ashton's forearm so hard pain coursed through his entire body. "What the *hell* was that?" he hissed through clenched teeth. "Are you out of your mind?"

"I'm righting a ten-year-old wrong, and there's nothing you can do to stop me."

"What does that mean? You're not making any sense."

"I was driving the night Mia died, and I'll do whatever

it takes to undo the harm you've caused, and make sure her reputation is restored."

To his surprise, Alexander looked relieved, not surprised, and Ashton suspected his dad was hiding something else from him. But what? What else could there be? Breaking free from his grasp, he stepped forward, determined to learn the truth. "Tell me everything."

"Ashton, honey, calm down." His mother stepped beside him. Her face wore a smile, but she sounded panicked. Her black, floor-length gown was simple, but elegant, and her diamond jewelry sparkled in the light of the moon. "What's going on? I can hear you shouting from across the yard."

"Dad lied about the car accident," Ashton said, struggling to control his temper. "Mia wasn't driving the night she died. I was, and Dad paid the police to cover it up."

Joan gasped. "Alexander, is that true? Did you do what Ashton's accusing you of?"

The silence was deafening.

"Say something," she snapped. "Don't just stand there. Explain yourself."

Alexander shoved his hands into his pants pocket, and shifted from one foot to the other.

Taking control of the situation, Joan linked arms with her husband and her son, and led them through the backyard. Her smile never wavered, but when they entered the house her façade cracked, and she exploded in anger. "Alexander, what did you do?" she demanded, propping her hands on her hips. "I have a right to know. I'm your wife."

"The less you know the better." Alexander reached into his jacket pocket and took out a hand-rolled cigar. "I did it for you, for all of us. The past is past, so leave it buried."

Ashton plucked the cigar out of his dad's mouth, broke it in half and tossed it on the kitchen counter. "The time for secrets is over, Dad. Come clean, or—"

"Risk losing your family forever," Joan added, narrowing her eyes. "I mean it this time, Alexander. If you don't confess, I'll leave you, and I won't come back."

Ashton held his breath, didn't move a muscle.

Alexander looked from one to the other, then nodded his head. One nod but it spoke volumes. "The day of the accident, I asked Mia to meet me at the office," he said, tugging at the collar of his Armani dress shirt. "I tried to pay her off, but she wouldn't take the money."

"You did what?" Ashton roared. "Why?"

Alexander scoffed. "Isn't it obvious? Mia Landers wasn't worthy of being our maid, let alone a Rollins, and I wasn't about to pass my legacy on to her. I offered her a million dollars to leave Miami and never return, but she refused. She left to see you at our estate."

"What happened when she got to the house?" Ashton asked. "Did we argue? Was she mad at me?"

"One of the housekeepers let her inside and told me later that Mia accused you of testing her loyalty. You denied it, and Mia rushed out of the house, inconsolable. You didn't want her driving, because she was distraught, and got behind the wheel to take her home."

Ashton was pissed, disgusted by his father's actions, but he listened intently to his story.

"The accident was just that—an accident—and since you woke up not remembering any of the events that led up to it, I thought it was best for everyone to think Mia had been driving. No one was hurt by it. Don't you see, Ashton? I did it to protect you."

"You did it to protect yourself!" Ashton fired back. "You paid off the police to falsify the accident reports and fabricate toxicology records, because you were afraid I'd find out you tried to bribe Mia to leave town. And when I questioned you about the accident in the hospital, you insisted on maintaining the lie."

"How could you?" Joan's voice wobbled, and anguish covered her face. "How could you purposely and willfully deceive our son? And ruin that poor girl's reputation?"

Alexander shrugged a shoulder, and it took every ounce of self-control Ashton had not to punch his father in the face. His thoughts were so dark they scared him. His mind was spinning, reeling from shock, and all he could think of was how much he needed to see Haley.

"I did what I thought was right at the time, and I have no regrets."

The air was thick, suffocating, making it hard for Ashton to breathe. His father's confession had cast a dark shadow over the anniversary party, ruining the festive occasion. Emotionally spent, Ashton wanted to go upstairs and lie down, but he knew if he abandoned his party his guests would be offended.

The French doors opened, and the noise from the backyard flooded the kitchen.

Haley entered the room, wearing an apologetic smile, and Ashton sighed in relief. She must have sensed his inner turmoil, because she walked over to him, clasped his hand and whispered, "Baby, everything's going to be okay. We'll get through this together. I promise."

Joan wiped her eyes and straightened her shoulders. "Son, we're leaving."

Too choked up to speak, Ashton merely nodded in response.

"Your father and I need to speak in private." Sniffling, Joan kissed him softly on the cheek. "I am so sorry…about everything… I didn't know."

Ashton watched his parents exit the kitchen and wondered if their marriage would survive. His father's demeanor was cold, his eyes lifeless, but his mother looked broken, as if her heart was in pieces, and Ashton sympathized with her.

"Sorry for interrupting," Haley said quietly. "But I got worried when you didn't return to the party and I wanted to check on you. I thought maybe you needed to vent."

Ashton told her about his conversation with his father. This time, he didn't hold back. He confided in Haley about his hurt, his anger and his animosity toward his dad. "My family is a mess," he said. "You should make a run for it while you still can, because things will probably never change."

"I'll take my chances. We're a team, Ashton, for better or worse."

"For better or worse?" he repeated, raising an eyebrow. "You'd marry me, knowing everything my father's done, and be willing to overlook his lies and deceit?"

"Ashton, baby, *you* did nothing wrong. Your fiancée died in a tragic car accident, and I'd never hold that against you." She wore an innocent expression on her face. "And as to whether or not I'd marry you, you'd have to ask me to find out."

They stared at each other for a long moment, and Ashton knew what he had to do. He felt compelled to bare his soul to her right then and there, in the middle of his kitchen. His pulse was pounding and his limbs were shaking, but he dropped to one knee and locked eyes with her. "You came into my life when I really needed a friend, and without your support I never would have survived the last two weeks."

Her face brightened, and Ashton knew his words pleased her.

"I love doing yoga with you, volunteering with you, traveling with you, and I want to spend the rest of my days and nights loving you." Ashton took her hand in his, lowered his mouth and kissed her palm. "You are everything I could ever want in a woman, and nothing would make me happier than being your husband. Haley Olivia Adams, will you marry me?"

"Of course I will! I love you more than anything, and you'll always have my heart."

Beaming, she cupped his face in her hands and gave him a sweet, soft peck on the lips. They kissed, clinging desperately to each other. Ashton had never felt more loved. He'd been given a second chance at love, and he was going to cherish her all the days of his life. His family was at odds, but as long as he had Haley, he could survive anything. And they would. Together.

Epilogue

"Congratulations to my daughter and my dashing new son-in-law on their marriage!" Careful not to spill her champagne, Melinda threw her arms around the happy couple, who were seated at the head of the table, and kissed them both on the cheek. "You two are a perfect match, and I hope your marriage is filled with love, joy and happiness—"

"May the honeymoon never end," Aunt Penny added with a playful wink.

Joan Rollins wagged a finger at the newlyweds. "I want grandbabies ASAP, or else!"

Everyone laughed, even the servers standing nearby, and Haley giggled.

Gazing at her new husband, Haley admired how sharp Ashton looked in his white Hugo Boss suit, silk tie and leather shoes. He was the love of her life, the best thing that had ever happened to her, and Haley hoped their children looked just like him.

Picking up her water glass, she saw her wedding ring twinkle in the sunshine. The one-of-a-kind emerald cut diamond was such a gorgeous piece of jewelry Haley couldn't stop staring at it. Ashton had enlisted the help of her mother to design the perfect ring, and knowing how much trouble he'd gone to to impress her made Haley love and appreciate him even more.

"Have I told you lately that I love you?" he whispered, brushing his nose against hers. "You're stunning, Haley, and I can't keep my hands off you."

His words and his gentle caress along her bare shoulders warmed her all over. Her lace headpiece was adorned with roses, diamonds shimmered in her ears and around her neck, and the intricate beadwork along the bodice of her strapless gown made her feel like a princess, and right now she was living the fairy tale.

"My life is full and rich because you're in it," he continued, "and I'm proud that you're my wife."

"Ashton, you've made me happier than I've ever been, and I love you so much I feel like I could burst," she confessed, a girlish smile overwhelming her mouth. "Thank you for being a man of integrity, and for taking such good care of me."

"And I always will. You're my everything, Haley, and I'll always put you first."

God, I love this man, she thought, gazing deep into his eyes. He means the world to me, and I'll never take him for granted.

Leaning in for a kiss, Haley brushed her lips slowly and tenderly against his mouth. Celebrating their nuptials in Ibiza with their family and friends was a dream come true, and Haley couldn't imagine a more perfect day. On their first date, Ashton had joked about taking her to the island for their honeymoon, and one year later he'd made good on his promise.

The scent of tropical fruit carried on the warm breeze, and Haley's mouth watered. With breathtaking views and a romantic ambience, the secluded island off the east coast of Spain was paradise on earth. Foregoing tradition, they'd decided to tie the knot at a five-star resort instead of at the family church in Miami. Mrs. Rollins had been disappointed, but once they told Joan they wanted a private, intimate ceremony for their one-year anniversary she'd given them her full support. They'd arrived on the island three days earlier, on the Rollins family jet, and the weekend had been filled with excitement and adventure. They'd taken a private boat tour, eaten sensational meals and enjoyed all of the amenities at the posh, upscale resort.

"I love you guys, and I'm so happy you found each other," Becca said, coming up to them with a bright smile on her face and hugging them both.

One by one, their guests offered toasts, best wishes and marital advice, which drew chuckles from Haley and Ashton. Wanting to avoid publicity, they'd kept the guest list small, choosing to invite only Daniel and Angela, Josh and Becca, Haley's parents and Ashton's mother. Alexander was back in Miami, and although it saddened Haley that her father-in-law wasn't in attendance she knew Ashton wasn't ready to let Alexander back into his life, and had respected his wishes. Still at odds with his father, Ashton didn't know if he'd ever be able to forgive his dad for what he did, but Alexander was doing what he could to provide restitution. The Aunt Penny Foundation had established a Mia Landers Memorial Scholarship that was being funded by the Rollins family, and Haley appreciated their generosity.

They posed for dozens of pictures, cut their five-tier vanilla-and-buttercream cake, and danced to song after song with their family and friends. Standing beside Ashton at the bar, sipping a glass of fruit punch, Haley listened as the conversation turned to the Prescott George organization and wondered if Ashton missed being president. Shortly after the anniversary party, he'd met with Joshua at his estate, and not only apologized for misjudging him, but pledged his support for his presidency. Once a week, Ashton had dinner with Daniel and Joshua, and now they were all good friends. Full of plans, Daniel and Joshua spoke openly about some of the challenges they faced as copresidents of the Miami chapter and of changes they hoped to implement nationwide.

"Interesting things are going on at the San Diego chapter," Daniel reported.

"Ashton, I know you'll be taking over as CEO of Rollins Aeronautics in the next week, but I'm hoping you can come with us to San Diego at the end of the month to lend a hand."

"Guys, count me in. I love the organization, and I'll do anything to help."

Daniel and Joshua left with cocktail glasses for their wives, leaving the newlyweds alone. Haley teased Ashton for acting like a bachelor and he wore an apologetic smile.

"Baby, I'm sorry. I wasn't thinking. I should have checked with you before agreeing to go to San Diego with Joshua and Daniel," he said, brushing a stray curl away from her face. "Do you have a problem with me staying active in the organization?"

"No, of course not. I know how much Prescott George means to you."

"That's my girl. I knew you'd understand. You always do."

"Just make sure you leave enough time for our family. I can't be raising your babies on my own. Babies are a lot of work, and I'm going to need your help, especially changing diapers."

"My *babies*?"

Haley nodded. The look on Ashton's face was priceless, and she giggled when his eyes widened and his jaw dropped. "Don't worry, I'm planning to have them one at a time."

"I'm going to be a daddy?" Ashton bellowed. "How long have you known?"

"Just a few weeks," she confessed. "It was hard keeping it a secret from you, but I thought it would make a nice wedding gift."

Whooping for joy, Ashton swept Haley off her feet and spun her around, oblivious to the curious expressions on the faces of their friends and family members.

"I love you, Mrs. Rollins."

Tears filled her eyes. "I love you, too, baby. More than you will ever know."

Inhaling his cologne, Haley draped her arms around his neck, and snuggled against his chest.

"A baby? I can hardly believe it. My mom is going to do backflips around the pool when she finds out!"

Laughing, Haley nodded in agreement.

"I've been thinking, maybe instead of building end tables for my home office, we can build a crib together instead."

"Great idea," Ashton said. "We'll get started on it as soon as we return to Miami."

Haley giggled. "Baby, relax. There's no rush. We have seven months before Ashton Jr. makes his grand entrance."

A proud smile filled his lips. "Thank you for the unexpected wedding gift. It's perfect. Just like you." To prove it, Ashton kissed Haley on the lips, then set off for their lavish honeymoon suite overlooking the beach, whistling the love song that was playing in his heart.

* * * * *

SPECIAL EXCERPT FROM

After scoring phenomenal success in Phoenix with her organic food co-op, Naomi Stallion is ready to introduce Vitally Vegan to her Utah town. But a nasty bidding war over the property Naomi wants to buy pits the unconventional lifestyle coach against sexy, überconservative corporate attorney Patrick O'Brien. When the stakes rise, will Patrick choose his career or the woman he yearns for?

Read on for a sneak peek at
SWEET STALLION,
the next exciting installment in author
Deborah Fletcher Mello's ***THE STALLIONS*** *series!*

Naomi shifted her gaze back to the stranger's, her palm sliding against his as he shook her hand. The touch was like silk gliding across her flesh, and she mused that he had probably never done a day's worth of hard labor in his life. "It's nice to meet you, Patrick," she answered. "How can we help you?"

"I heard you mention the property next door. Do you mind sharing what you know about it?"

She looked him up and down, her mind's eye assembling a photographic journal for her to muse over later. His eyes were hazel, the rich shade flecked with hints of gold and green. He was tall and solid, his broad chest and thick arms pulling the fabric of his shirt taut. His jeans fit comfortably

KPEXP0817

against a very high and round behind, and he had big feet. Very big feet in expensive, steel-toed work boots. He exuded sex appeal like a beacon. She hadn't missed the looks he was getting from the few women around them, one of whom was openly staring at him as they stood there chatting.

"What would you like to know about Norris Farms?" Naomi asked. She crossed her arms over her chest, the gesture drawing attention to the curve of her cleavage.

Patrick's smile widened. "Norris," he repeated. "That's an interesting name. Is it a fully functioning farm?"

"It is. They use ecologically based production systems to produce their foods and fibers. They are certified organic."

"Is there a homestead?"

"There is."

"Have the owners had it long? Is there any family history attached to it?"

Naomi hesitated for a brief second. "May I ask why you're so interested? Are you thinking about bidding on this property?"

Patrick clasped his hands behind his back and widened his stance a bit. "I'm actually an attorney. I represent the Perry Group and they're interested in acquiring this lot."

Both Naomi and Noah bristled slightly, exchanging a quick look.

Naomi scoffed, apparent attitude evident in her voice. "The Perry Group?"

Patrick nodded. "Yes. They're a locally owned investment company. Very well established, aren't they?"

Her eyes narrowed as she snapped, "We know who they are."

Don't miss SWEET STALLION
by Deborah Fletcher Mello, available September 2017
wherever Harlequin® Kimani Romance™
books and ebooks are sold!

KPEXP0817